I0653105

The Young Novelist

JASMIN ROSE

JASMIN ROSE PUBLISHING

Contents

For my family and friends-

Thank You!

I love you all! xx

Author Notes

Hi Lovely Reader!

Thank you for taking the time to read **The Young Novelist**, your support means the world to me!

Before you begin your reading journey with Emma in Kingship Valley, I would like to explain a few key points that are within this novel.

- The use of telegrams are purely for fun. I am aware that they were not a primary or preferred form of communication, but I feel like it was fitting for this to be included in Emma's journey.

- Emma refers to herself as a novelist, yes, technically she works as a journalist, but she has hopes to become a novelist. She refers to herself as a novelist to motivate herself, to encourage herself, and to keep hope that she will one day achieve this goal.

- Emma needs to be mindful and careful about how many feminist articles she releases throughout the book. They have been spaced out. She needs to maintain her job at the newspaper to ensure her writing goals. So, bombarding the storyline with feminist articles wouldn't have benefited the storyline or Emma.

With these key points in mind, I strongly encourage you to have fun while reading this! I had so much fun writing it!

Much love,

Jasmin

Chapter One

I am a novelist. I am a feminist. I am human.

I love looking towards the stars and wishing upon them. Today, I wish that my family would return home.

This time, my family left to visit a relative in Queensland three days ago. Fortunately, I was left home to look after the place. The house was always kept clean, Ma is a massive clean freak. Nothing was ever out of place, everything has it's spot and place in the house, and nothing new was ever welcome. I adored staying home alone, sitting by the fire reading, feeling the warm heat against my cold cheeks. Nothing beats sitting by the fire, coffee in hand, with a novel being pressed against the palm of my hand...nothing.

'Emma? Are you home?' a voice called from the front door.

'I'm coming, Brendan!' I called back. 'What can I do for you?' I continued once I reached the door.

'I was wondering if you would like to go for a walk?' he asked with a small, goofy smile.

'Sorry, I am currently in the middle of something'

'Like what? Reading?'

'Yes, and that is what I plan to do with my days, so please' I said, shooing him away.

'What are you reading?' he asked.

'Only one of the best novels ever written' I replied, dramatically, to emphasise my point.

'Which is?'

'*Little Women*, of course!' I replied, a matter of fact.

'Didn't you say the same thing last week about *Romeo and Juliet*?'

'Yes, another well-written novel. You should try reading sometimes. You never know what you will find within a good book'

'I don't need to read. I am fine just the way I am'

'Sure, if you say so...now if you don't mind, I would like to get back to reading'

'Of course, we will hang out another time, Em. If there is ever a time you aren't reading or writing'

'That would be very doubtful. I will always be reading and writing. Sorry to disappoint. Now if you don't mind, I have business to attend to'

'Have fun reading, Em,' he replied before I closed the door.

Why do men need to be so difficult? Can't he just under-stand where I am coming from? Reading is pure gold, how can he not see that? I thought to myself as I made my way back to the fireplace, back to my novel.

As the warm bliss from the fireplace warmed the chilled winter air, I thought about my career. What I wanted to do in the new year. I hadn't a clue. My love for the written language has always been strong, overpowering, and loving. I always saw myself as the next *Jane Austen.* Someone who was not afraid to speak up about women's empowerment and rights through her works. Something that I only wished I could be. While my written works might not be as accomplished as *Jane Austen* I just hoped that the stories that I will be telling change lives and the way people think about themself and others.

'This book is incredible!' I exclaimed excitedly to myself.

Maybe it might be a good idea for me to go and write more? I mean, I have almost finished Little Women for the fourteenth time. I thought to myself as I rose and headed towards my room, a small room containing one bookshelf filled to the brim with books, a small writing desk stationed near the window with her typewriter, and a mountain of written works and progression works waiting idly for me to start writing again, a bed stationed near the wall opposite to my desk. While I didn't own much, I loved my life and my room. I had everything I would ever need.

I fell in love with reading and writing at a very young age. My Ma gifted me some old books which included authors such as *Jane Austen, Emily Brontë, Charlotte Brontë,* and lastly *Louisa May Alcott*. While I currently don't know what I want to do I dreamed of becoming a successful author, inspiring young women, and sharing my love for words and storytelling.

'Right, where to start?' I asked myself while I set up my typewriter.

'Ah yes... that would work'

Once upon a time there lived a Princess. This princess was betrothed to a King, however, the Princess was unhappy. You see she didn't need or want to marry a King, in fact she didn't want to marry at all. This was all her father's doing. If you don't marry someone before your 22nd birth-day you are then classified as a witch and would be killed or imprisoned for studies. Something in which I didn't want to find out. While my life is *basic, and easy. And I don't dislike the King, but I certainly don't love him. If I did have a choice in who I would marry, it would be to someone who loved me in return, no questions asked. Just pure love. While I can see the King does love me to some extent, he certainly would much rather marry someone else. I don't even know what love feels like, but I imagine it to be amazing, and splendid and make me feel warm and happy inside.*

If you were wondering, I am known as Princess Julieanne. I have been called noble, brave, loyal, and lov-ing. But I am unhappy with my life and what people have chosen for me. All I really want is freedom. To be able to choose how I live my own life and not have to worry about people's opinions. And as I am a princess, everyone looks up to me and admires me. This makes my life so hard, I always need to be on my best, gracious behaviour. It's silly really, but I do what I must to ensure that my people are happy with me and that they want me to rule them. If the people decide that they don't want me as their Queen once I marry the King, then this can cause rifts within the region, something that we cannot afford to do.

My kingdom is the largest in the world, therefore it needs more maintenance and rules. The rulers cannot be random people, they have to be born royal, like the current King. Or chosen by the King or the King's father in some cases, from wealthy, well-known, and respected families, such as my own. You see, my father is the best friend of the former King, King George. The current King, my *future husband, is King Phillips. Our Kingdom is known as the Northwind. Besides Northwind being the largest kingdom, it is also the most respected and feared. We have the best warriors, due to size, but also because of their skill sets. We have the best assassins, guards, and trainers but also the best doctors, nurses, and psychics. Most kingdoms have thieves, murderers, rogue groups, liars, and manipulators that try to change the kingdom's hierarchy and laws, Northwind is no different…*

***

The Winter Wonderland Festival

Each year members from the local town host an annual 'Winter Wonderland Festival', this festival is a competition between all of the local towns.

The winner gets written down in the compendium, going down in the history books. This festival encourages towns to better their community and allows people to interact with each other. This also gives the towns a chance to interact and challenge each other, this is purely a fun event.

The running winner over the past couple of years is Kahibi. Reigning for 3 years now.

Most towns have activities for everyone, children and parents.

Some of the activities include,

- Barbeques

- Hide and seek arena

- Horse riding

. Sheep shearing

And many more, the town with the most
visitors and attractions wins, you
will need to create an event that
excites the town and encourages new
people to visit the town. Giving the
towns a chance to meet new people and
encourage them to come back.

This festival will be featured in
national newspapers to ensure the
nation knows about it.

All towns beware, I believe that
Kingship Valley is going to win this
year! But good luck to you all either
way!

I can't wait to see what this year's
Winter Wonderland Festival will bring

```
to our beautiful towns and what new
connections we will all make.
```

```
Written by,

Emma Hicks
```

Ring...ring...ring...

'Hello,' I spoke into the telephone.

'Emma?' spoke the voice on the other end of the line.

'Yes...? Who is this?' I asked nervously.

'It's Ben, can I come over to talk?'

'About what?'

'I'll explain once I get there...please?'

'Sure'

'Thank you...' he replied, leaving me greeted by silence on the other end of the line, like an abyss waiting for my arrival.

CHAPTER TWO

'Ben, what do I owe the pleasure?' I said as I answered my door.

'It's freezing outside, how are you in a dress?' he replied.

'The fire is lit. What did you need to speak to me about?'

'I have been offered a job in Melbourne, I'm thinking about taking it'

'Melbourne? What will you be doing?'

'Working as a sale's marketer and writing reviews of products'

'Nice, I guess there isn't any big companies around here'

'Definitely not, besides I think it would be a good change' he replied as he took a seat in front of the fire.

'Would you like some tea? Or coffee?'

'Coffee please'

'I'll be right back' I reply before heading to the kitchen.

Melbourne...that's so far away! I'd have to send him a telegram weekly! I am going to miss him so much. I thought to myself as I made the coffee for Ben and myself.

'What do you think about my job offer?' Ben inquired once I returned with the coffee in hand.

'I think that it is a great opportunity'

'You do?'

'Of course! Why wouldn't I?'

'Because you didn't seem happy when I told you about it, is all'

'Yes...well you caught me off-guard. But honestly, it is a great offer. It will give you the opportunity to practice reviews and get your name out into the world, you wouldn't have accomplished anything here anyway, so why not venture to the major cities?'

'I guess that makes sense, so you aren't mad?'

'No, I am happy for you. I knew this town wouldn't be able to hold you down forever'

'But you wanted it too'

'No, I want you to succeed, but I don't want you to leave me behind, so I will be sending you weekly telegrams'

'That cost will add up, you don't need to send them weekly'

'I know, but I want to—'

Knock...knock...

'Coming!' I called as I made my way to the door.

'Hey' acknowledges Brendan as I open the door.

'Hello, if you want me to go out again, I can't. I have a guest'

'Who?'

'Ben'

'May I come in?'

'Sure' I replied as I held open the door, allowing him to enter the house.

'I am guessing he is here to tell you about his job offer?'

'Yes...'

'Cool. Hey, Ben'

'Hey, Brendan. What's up?'

'The sky?'

'Wow, you are so funny!' I exclaimed sarcastically.

'I thought so, Em,' he replied, smirking at her.

'So...Brendan, have you got anything exciting planned?'

'No, currently not. My current goal, well only goal, is to get Em out of this house and into reality. With real people and conversations'

'Well, I think that Emma is doing a great job, she is exploring novels and learning about the world through them. It saves having to travel and not to mention saving money in the process'

'Thank you, Ben. I knew you would understand'

'Always, Emma. That's why I'm your best friend, remember?'

'Second best' interrupts Brendan.

'Actually, no. Ben is my best friend, B. Sorry to disappoint'

'Not disappointing at all, I know I'm also important to you'

'Yes, of course you are,' I replied with a small smile.

'Well, I best be off. I have to tell a couple more people about my job offer, and get their opinions. I am glad you understand, Emma' explained Ben.

'Good luck! Keep me updated!' I replied.

'Of course I will, goodbye Brendan. Don't get Emma into any trouble in my absence'

'You won't be leaving for a couple of days yet, so I wouldn't until after that point'

'Actually, I wish you luck convincing her to do anything that could even remotely get her into trouble' he continues before hugging me and heading to the door. 'Talk soon, Emma' he continued before closing the door leaving Brendan and I alone.

'So...Em, how is your book coming along?' asked Brendan as he walked over and placed his hands on my waist.

'I have almost finished reading *Little Women*' I replied as I placed my hands around his neck drawing his face towards mine, resulting in a very sweet kiss.

'We need to go out on another date' whines Brendan as he pulls away an inch.

'I know, and we will. But not today, B...ok?' I ask.

'Ok...tomorrow night, I'm coming to get you at around 5:30, you are mine for the night. Deal?'

'Fine, I will write my book during the day'

'That sounds like a great plan' he replied before kissing me once more, deeper this time. Eagerly. Passionately.

We stand there arm in arm, kissing until the firelight dims and is barely lighting the small room. Until the sun has completely set. Until night takes over the town.

'B' I murmured against his lips.

'Yes?' he murmured back.

I pull away to look into his eyes, before saying 'I think I might want you to stay over and hug me while I sleep'

'I think I would love to do that' he replies before placing a kiss to my forehead and grabbing my hand leading me towards my room, my bed.

We lay there in silence, my head on his chest, before sleep enveloped me into a dream filled slumber.

***

Waking up to the smell of coffee is the best thing ever! And the best thing is, I am not the one making it...Brendan...my hero.

'Ah good, you're awake' waltzed in Brendan, elegantly, coffee in hand.

'Yep...is that mine?' I replied, eyeing the coffee.

'Sure is...' he replied before placing a kiss on my forehead.

'Did you sleep well?' I asked.

'Of course, I had the best company'

'I'm glad. What are your plans for today?'

'To spend time with you...unless you have other plans?'

'Nope, I was just going to continue writing my book'

'Sounds like a nice plan'

'Indeed it is'

'Well, I'm going to go to the markets. Would you like me to get you anything?'

'No, thank you. I think I already have everything I need for the next couple of days'

'Awesome, well, I'll be back here later' he replied as he placed a soft, delicate kiss on my lips.

'Sounds like a plan' I replied before I kissed him again before he turned away and headed for the door.

Damn, I love him so much. I thought as I made my way to the living room.

I lit the fire, put away the dishes and placed *Little Women* on my chair. Ready to read later on today. But first, my book needs to be written more on.

After taking a seat at my writing desk, I set to work. I had big dreams for this novel, but first I needed to finish it.

***

'Northwind is one of the most feared and respected kingdoms in all of the lands, Julieanne. Why can't you accept the fact that you will be their Queen and that there are expectations

that must be upheld to?' asked my
Father.

'But Father, I understand all of those
things. But surely there is a maiden
somewhere in Northwind that would be
more suitable to be Queen?' I asked.

'No, I am the Former King's trusted
friend. We are held at high standards
within Northwind, there is no other
maiden that would be suitable to be
Queen. There is no other maiden that
is even friends or associated with
the royal family besides yourself.
You and King Phillips are going to
rule with grace and dignity, you are
going to make both our families proud.
Every maiden in Northwind would do
anything to be in your position. My
darling, I understand that you don't
want to marry and I understand that
if you were to marry then you would
want it to be for love, but it just
isn't possible'

'Is it possible? Or just not what you and the Former King want?'

'Julieanne…please just get ready for the ceremony. You mustn't be late' my Father sighed before exiting my chambers.

Right, how hard can it be to accept the crown and become Queen? I thought to myself.

The dress that was selected for the coronation included an elegant sky blue, long gown with a small blue tiara. The blue tiara is the Princesses current crown to signify who she is to everyone, all of the royal Princesses have a colour that matches them. Julieanne has a blue theme about her, therefore any formal occasions she is always paired up with blue. Her Queen crown will also be blue.

```
'Julieanne? Are you ready to begin?'
asked her personal maid, Roseanne.

'Yes, I will be out shortly' I
replied.
```

***

Ring...ring...ring...

'Hello?' I asked through the telephone.

'Hello, darling. I have just gotten back in range for a telephone call. However, I don't have long. How are you going?' she asked.

'I'm doing well thanks, Ma. It won't be long until you are home now'

'Definitely not. How are things with the house?'

'All clean, just like how you left it'

'Perfect. What have you been doing?'

'Writing and reading, Ma'

'Like always. Have you had anyone over?'

'Yes, Ben and Brendan'

'Ok...I like those two. They don't mess up my house. Have you been out anywhere?'

'No, Brendan and I are going out later this afternoon, but I shall not be out late'

'That's fine, darling. well...I must be getting going. Your sister says hi too and so does your father'

'I say hello back, I love you. Safe travels'

'We love you too, Emma. We will be home before you know it'

'Can't wait' I replied before disconnecting the telephone.

I often missed my family, but I also loved the peace and quiet when they weren't around, especially when May-belle wasn't around. That girl can make the whole town run and hide when she is in a talkative mood. She wants to become a famous singer. She is only thirteen, she has a long way to go before she can leave home and pursue her dreams. Not like Ma would ever let her leave, or Pa for that matter. I am the oldest daughter, therefore I was left at home to look after the house, which I loved to do.

*Right, I think it might be time to sit by the fire and write a telegram for Grandmother...*I thought as I made my way to the lounge room and sat down on my chair.

Dearest Grandmother,

I am sorry I haven't written to you for a while, I have been busy writing and reading while the family are away. I am so sorry to hear about Grandfather, he will be forever missed. Unfortunately, myself and the family currently don't have the funds to go to the funeral given that you are in the US and we are in Australia. If we had the money then we would definitely travel to visit. Please send a telegram if there is anything that you need from us. I am always around to talk. I wish you lived closer so I could see you...I have not seen you in months since you last visited us, I am always going to look forward to your visit. And it is well worth the wait.

How are your cleaner and nurse treating you? Focus on getting through the next couple of weeks, and remember that there is always at least one positive thing every day. I try to think of one daily, it is possible. If you need to speak to someone, please speak to your nurse or caretaker, they can either help you or redirect you to someone else. I hope Max is well, he has always been a good dog to you.

Ma, Pa, Maybelle, and I send you all the love in the world, we all wish you were here with us. Maybelle is having her thirteenth birthday in three days, she is so excited. I am still writing my novel about Princess Julieanne and her life, which is progressing well. I hope someday you will get to read it. I think you would really love Princess Julieanne and her lifestyle. Ma is starting work at the sewing foundation, they have requested for some seamstresses to help make children's clothes, Ma *jumped at the opportunity. Pa is continuing to work at the mines, even when we have all begged him to stop. It is just too dangerous, but Pa argues and states that it is worth the wage. If you ever could try and convince your son to retire or leave the mines, please do so. Maybe he will listen to you. Hopefully. Oh, and Maybelle has also started singing lessons which she is loving, and she is starting to tutor younger children so she has the funds to pay for her lessons. I will begin editing writing materials from the school kids as well as writing for the local newspaper. The newspaper owner has told me that my writing is too good for a small town such as ours. But for now, Kingship Valley will be the only place that hears my stories and writing.*

As mentioned in our last telegram, I will write you a line from my novel.

It says,

'Once upon a time, there lived a Princess. This princess was betrothed to a King, however, the Princess was unhappy. You see she didn't need or want to marry a King, in fact, she didn't want to marry at all. This was all her father's doing. If you don't marry someone before your 22nd birthday you are then classed as a witch and would be killed or imprisoned for studies. Something that I didn't want to find out. While my life is basic and easy.'

That is part of the starting paragraph, I hope you like it. Yes, I know it is a typical way to start a happily ever after story, however, I think it is the perfect way to start mine off. It will fit in well with the storyline.

I must conclude this telegram, otherwise, it will be too long to post.

I hope everything is well with you and I look forward to our next visit.

Remember, think about the positives every day, don't just focus on the negatives.

Love,

Emma Hicks

I love writing to my Grandmother, however, I never want to end it. I could just keep writing it all out, but of course, I can't.

'Em, are you home?' called Brendan from the front door.

'Coming B!' I called back as I made my way to let him inside.

'Hello, darling' he smiled before placing a soft kiss on my lips.

'Hey' I replied 'Come in' I continued as I moved out of his way.

'What have you gotten up to?' he asked, placing his bags on the kitchen counter.

'I wrote more on my novel, set the fire, tidied the house, and wrote Gran a telegram'

'Sounds productive. Have you gotten any more writing tasks from the newspaper?'

'No, I am due to write one tomorrow and send it in for publication next week. But I am still waiting on the topic and the supporting evidence'

'That's frustrating, but I am sure you will be awesome'

'Thanks' I smiled in return to his grin. 'How were the markets?' I continued.

'Surprisingly busy. I think the town over from ours is having some sort of celebration. There are a lot of people from out of town, too many for just visiting our town'

'That's strange, I haven't heard about it. Generally, I write articles and promotional stuff for the newspaper'

'Maybe they published it in the national newspaper'

'I guess...'

'I am sure that you will get the chance to give an overview of it, one of those around here really reads the national newspaper, there is no real point since we have our own newspaper, and our newspaper is also shared with our surrounding towns. Therefore you also get to write about their towns as well as ours'

'Yeah, I guess so'

'I should probably tidy up my writing desk though. Otherwise, I won't know where to look for my things. I'll be back out shortly'

'Good, because it is time for our picnic'

'Can't wait'

Right, I need to quickly write out a to-do list, otherwise, I'll forget about it. I thought after I sorted out my desk.

I then grabbed a piece of paper and started writing out my to-do list.

<u>To-Do:</u>

- ~~Tidy up the writing desk~~

- Tidy up kitchen

- ~~Write a telegram to send to Grandmother~~

- Write a telegram to send to Uncle Mick

- Send off Grandmother and Uncle Mick's telegram

- Clean out the fireplace and tidy the living room

- Start writing articles for the newspaper

- ~~Edit my novel and continue writing it~~

- Buy more coffee, biscuits, and tea

- ~~Make bed~~

- ~~Sort out clothes~~

- Put washing on the line

- Clean dishes

Perfect, that should keep me busy for the next couple of days.
I thought on my way out to Brendan.

'Ready to go?' he asked.

'Of course,' I replied.

CHAPTER THREE

'This is nice' I commented while I leaned against Brendan's shoulder looking out over the town. The perfect picnic location in all of Kingship Valley.

'Yeah it is, and I have the best company in the world' Brendan replied with a smile while leaning in and kissing me on the forehead.

'I am sure your Ma would disagree,' I replied.

'True, she, for some reason, thinks that she is the best company in town. But we will let her think that. She doesn't need to know or hear the truth'

'I am sure your Ma does make the best company at certain times'

'She does, especially since Pa left'

'Have you heard from him?' I asked.

'No, but I am sure Brisbane is treating him well. There are more girls there'

'Your Pa wasn't all bad, he did love you'

'You don't leave and ignore someone you love, that is not how it works'

'Maybe not to you, but maybe he is working through some stuff' I reply, now sitting up to face him.

'But it was also *his* choice to leave, not mine, not Ma's, *his*'

'I get that, but I do hope that there is a reasonable explanation for it, then you and your Ma can get some closure'

'Doubtful, but I do hope Ma finds the strength to move on and get back up'

'How is she doing?'

'The same as before. Weeping around the house, in her pajamas, messy hair with red puffy eyes'

'Poor thing, I should make some brownies and take them to her tomorrow'

'I think she would love a visit from you, but she hasn't been eating recently, therefore there is no point in making brownies. Maybe bring some of your homemade tea, the one that makes everyone in town feel better?'

'My 'get well soon' tea?' I laughed.

'Yeah, that one' he replied, laughing.

'I will bring a cart full' I replied smiling.

'I love you'

'I love you more, B' I replied while running my hand down his chest.

'*I doubt that*' he whispered while leaning in to place a kiss on my lips, passionately, carefully, lovingly.

As we lay there watching the sky change colours, from day to dusk, to nightfall. The most beautiful times of the day end and repeat. Day in, day out, but it never is the same, and it is never not beautiful. Brendan and I lay in silence watching the ever-changing sky, like they can see all their dreams and wishes coming true in them like the only thing that matters is them in this moment of peace.

'I love the stars,' I whispered, afraid to break the blissful silence enveloping them.

'They glow eternally, just like you' Brendan whispered back.

'I wish there was a world, where the stars shine all day, every day. Eternal night. The stars hold dreams and hopes. I wish there was a world where the stars made all of the wishes and dreams come true, that people would wish upon them and dream about them. Every one of the wishes and dreams made upon a star was to come true'

'You could include that in your novel, it sounds magical'

'It would be'

'Am I in your novel?'

'I guess, I think that the king represents you in some way'

'I'm glad, does that mean Julieanne represents you? In some way?'

'I guess, but I'm not too sure, she more reminds me of Maybelle'

'You're writing a character based on your younger sister?'

'I guess'

'That's cute'

'Yeah...' I sighed 'I think it might be time to head home and get some rest'

'I think so too'

***

'Hello?' I responded as I answered the telephone the following morning.

'Good morning, Emma. This is Edwardson from the Newspaper. How are you?' he replies.

'I'm well thank you, do you have something that you would like me to write about?'

'Yes, I actually do. There was a festival last night in Kahibi. They have requested it be written about in our next newspaper. I have sent a runner boy to you, he will have the information that we would like to be included in the article. I must be going now Emma, I look forward to reading about it'

'Ok, thank you Edwardson' I replied as the line went dead.

Just as I was about to return to my seat in front of the fireplace I heard a knock at the front door.

Oh, this must be the runner boy that Edwardson mentioned he sent. I thought as I made my way to the front door. *That was quick.*

'Hello, are you Emma?' asked the young boy.

'I am'

'Edwardson has asked me to give this to you, he wants a draft before tomorrow night also as he wants to publish it on Tuesday' the boy explained.

'Thank you' I smiled before shutting the door and heading for my room to start my first draft.

The letter that I received read;

Dear Emma,

We are under the understanding that you are the best novelist in the area. With this in mind, we have personally requested that you write an article on the festivities that took place in Kahibi last night. I will write out the events below for your reference, whilst we generally share our festivities with your company, we have begun going to larger companies for wider media reach. However, pending the story that you write, we might just stay within your company, within your reach. After all, the better the writer, the better the story. Good luck in writing this article, I look forward to reading it.

A basic outline of the festivities from last night.

- *Kids horse riding, water fight, face painting, and petting zoo.*

- *At 5:30 there was a supper ceremony.*

- *6 pm fireworks*

- *7 pm camp fire, spooky stories*

Please be mindful that this is an outline of key events from the night, please include quotes and other things that you have heard or that are included inside my other note. Make these festivities land on the front page! This festival was in honor of our town turning 50 years old, so this was a big festival for our town, therefore, it should be an important factor of the newspaper.

Please write this well...

Yours sincerely,

Mr. A Whitington

With all of this information in place, I set to work on my article. With high hopes of putting it on the front page of the newspaper.

***

The Town Of Kahibi Turns 50!

The town's president, Mr. A Whitington celebrates with his fellow community of their beautiful, small town turning 50 years old!

Mr. A Whitington reports that 'This festival was the largest our town has ever had! I am very pleased to be the president during these proud times'. In regards to Mr. A Whitington's report, we have other reports saying that this festival brought the most people out to our area in years, this is beneficial not just for Kahibi but also for all of our towns, putting us on the map!

The town of Kahibi celebrated this massive occasion with fireworks, bonfires, horse riding, a petting zoo, face painting, and of course spooky stories! This festival was a great way for families to get out of the house and celebrate an amazing occasion. 'Happy kids equals a happy household' as my parents like to say.

Kahibi is known for its loving, nurturing, welcoming environment, a great place for kids! Kahibi has the best wine estate in all of New South Wales, all of the local towns get their supply of wine from their beautiful estate. Some say the reason it is the best is because it is made from love, and I 100% agree!

A fellow reporter commented on the festivities last night saying, 'Wow, it is such an honor to be reporting here, in Kahibi on the day it turns 50 years old! The festivities are so amazing and not to mention fun! While I stand here reporting on this amazing occasion all I can see are happy families, a happy town. Definitely worth the visit!'. This reporter only touches base on what an amazing event the festival is and what an amazing place Kahibi is.

While I can most certainly rave about how great Kahibi is, I am a writer, I write the truth. And I write what I know. Mr. A Whitington is an amazing president, he has changed Kahibi in so many ways and continues to make it a better place for everyone. Since I missed the festivities myself, I have gotten a couple of community members to write to me explaining what they loved about the festivities.

'I loved the food!', 'The kids had a blast! I can't wait for another!', 'I was invited by my mother to visit Kahibi for the festival, I am so glad I did! It surely beats the city festivals by far! Everyone is so loving and supportive!', 'This was my little boy's first time in Kahibi and he doesn't want to leave!'

While I can continue adding quotes and comments, I believe you get the hint. Yes, you should visit Kahibi! Yes, it is the best town around here! Yes, everyone loves visitors! Yes, you can try the amazing wine!

```
So please next time you are around,
stop by and say 'Hi!', I am sure Mr.
A Whitington would love to hear from
you!


Written by;

Emma Hicks
```

***

Dear Mr. A Whitington,

It has been an absolute honour writing about your town and its festival! I hope you enjoy what I have written. I have just posted it to my publisher. It should be published in our next paper on Tuesday morning, while it may not reach your town until Wednesday morning, it will definitely be in there. Your festival sounds amazing! I am so sorry I missed it! I am looking forward to writing more about your town and its events. Please feel free to reach out in the future if

you have anything else you would like me to write about, and
please let me know your thoughts on the story!

I hope my story touches many hearts, and that more people
will visit your amazing town, and in the process, visit my
own. Since we are neighboring towns we need to support each
other.

Yours sincerely;

Emma Hicks

***

Right, I will need to do the laundry tomorrow, running out
of sunlight today. Maybe I can do the washing up today. I
thought as I made my way to the kitchen.

I have always loved to clean and tidy the house, I must have
gotten it from Ma. She is always cleaning too. My room is
always tidy, everything has a place. I don't, generally, buy

new things, and when I do it is usually the same item that I am replacing with a newer version such as my writing paper.

With the washing up done and dusted, I decided that I would clean out the fireplace. I loved cleaning out the fireplace, but I always needed to wear old clothes. The ash gets everywhere! But I remind myself every time that the fireplace needs to be cleaned so I can use it. Something I do often. Once I was finished with the fireplace and tidying up the lounge room I returned to the kitchen and prepped for supper, while that was cooking I headed back to my room where I could cross things off my to-do list and see if there was anything else that I could do.

To-Do:

- ~~Tidy up the writing desk~~

- Tidy up kitchen

- ~~Write a telegram to send to Grandmother~~

- Write a telegram to send to Uncle Mick

- Send off Grandmother and Uncle Mick's telegram

- ~~Clean out the fireplace and tidy the living room~~

- ~~Start writing articles for the newspaper~~

- ~~Edit my novel and continue writing it~~

- Buy more coffee, biscuits, and tea

- ~~Make bed~~

- ~~Sort out clothes~~

- Put washing on the line

- ~~Clean dishes~~

Once I have finished with supper, I will clean the kitchen. But for the time being, I will write out my telegram to Uncle Mick, ready to post out first thing tomorrow morning. I thought.

Dearest Uncle Mick,

I hear that you are unwell again. This is the fifth time this year and it's only July! How many times can one person get sick? I am sorry that we are unable to be there for you every time you get sick, please continue to visit the doctors. Yes, I know you don't like to go to the doctor, but it is just something that you need to do.

I am writing to fill you in on myself and the family. I am sure you are aware that the family is currently away, they sent their condolences and hope you are feeling better soon.

My writing career is the same as before, I have started helping out the local businesses in creating promotions, and I have also begun making and selling my teas again. They were popular and more than one person has now approached me and requested an order, so I cannot disappoint them. I currently have some of my 'get well soon' in production, Brendan's mother is having a hard time, her husband left during the night and hasn't returned, leaving a note saying that he won't be coming home and that he has moved to begin a new life. This made the whole family sad, but Bren-

dan's mother seems to have taken it the worst, B is just angry about it all. I don't blame him. He is being so supportive of his mother, I don't know what she would be without him.

Anyway, I hope you are well soon, Uncle Mick.

We are all sending you hugs and kisses, please reach out again if there is anything you need.

Love,

Emma Hicks

Right, with that out of the way. Supper should be ready by now. Then I can clean the kitchen, have a shower, and write more in my book. Great plan. I thought.

CHAPTER FOUR

'I now pronounce you Queen of North-wind!' exclaimed the priest.

Wow, I didn't expect everything to go so smoothly, I thought something was bound to happen on my coronation.

'Darling?' interrupted King Phillips.

'Yes?' I replied.

'Do you care to dance?'

'Yes'

As we danced, all my worries dis-
appeared into nothingness. I was at
peace with the life that was chosen
for me to live, well at least for
now. Being Queen will bear a lot of
challenges and dilemmas.

'What are you thinking about, darling?' asked King Phillips as we
waltzed around the elegantly decorated ballroom.

'I am thinking about how peaceful this
all is and how challenging it will be
to become the perfect queen for our
people'

'Oh please! Challenging? You have
been acting like a queen since we were
both children, therefore it isn't
much different for you than being a
Princess'

'Queen Julieanne?' interrupted Father.

'Yes, Father?'

'Congratulations, that wasn't so bad now was it?'

'No, it wasn't. Are you here to say 'I told you so'?'

'Of course not! I have come to congratulate you both, you will make an amazing King and Queen. Now if you guys need me I'll be over with the Former King, we have some arrangements to plan'

'Of course, you guys do, I wouldn't expect anything else from you both'

As the party came to an end I caught myself wondering what it would be like to be normal, after tonight going back down to the village, sitting by

the fireplace, and reading a book
to the children. Of course, I can
do that here but I think it would
be different. I think it would be
more appreciated. Nothing would be
taken for granted, it sounds magical.
While I don't mean to take things for
granted, I believe I probably still
do.

                        ***

I like that. I thought as I rose from my chair, gathering
my telegrams and bag. Ready to head down and post them
out.

"Ello, Emma, 'ave you been writing lately?' asked the post-
man.

'Always, Jerry. How are you and the family?'

'Good, good. Our youngest off to school next year'

'Oh, nice! I'm sure you are all very excited about that'

''er Ma don't want 'er to go'

'No Ma ever does, well at least mine didn't either'

'That is two. But sure others wouldn't either. I shall 'ave these sent for you, Emma'

'Thanks, Jerry. I don't know what I'd do without you'

''ave a nice day'

'I will thanks, same to you'

'I shall' he replies before jumping onto his tricycle and heading off to do his morning rounds.

Once I returned home, I set to work checking my own mail. Something I needed to do on a daily basis to ensure that I didn't miss any writing jobs.

Thankfully, there was no important mail. Now I just needed to put my teas into their jars, ready for people to buy and collect.

***

'Emma? Are you ready to go?' called Brendan from the hallway.

'Yes, let's go' I called back.

'Ma is going to love seeing you, it will brighten up her mood for a little while'

'I can't wait to see her, I haven't seen her in forever. I hope she likes my tea bundle'

'I'm sure she would love it'

'I hope so...'

The walk to Brendan's is always a relaxing one, such a familiar one too. Since most of the town lives on properties, most families supply food products, produce, and other things such as candles, soap, clothing, blankets, coal, and freshwater although technically it's collected rainwater as well as tank water that gets delivered once a week. So most families use their water very sparingly. Nothing is ever wasted, which is great. The compost from our food goes into the gardens or crops to help them grow. The water from bathing is then reused for washing hands. Once the water has become useless in terms of cleaning hands, it is then used to clean the toilet. Since most families cannot afford proper plumbing, most things are done via a bucket. Every family contributes to the community in one way or another, and most children don't move out of town. They stay and help run the family business with their parents and then they take over the business once their parents have passed on. It is very rare for any child to move out of town, and those that have always come back within the first year. Ben is the first person to leave town this year, and he is the only one who is leaving and going to work in a big city company.

My family has been in this town for generations. Grandmother is the first person, ever, in our town's history to move overseas. This is something that she had always wanted to do, so she did. She is now in Kingship Valley's history books, something that my family has always been in. I am the best writer in town, in our history. Anything that needs to be written, I get asked to write, this includes from all of the other towns. I get telegrams daily about things that they want me to write about. I write more for everyone else than for myself.

This morning, for example, I had three telephone calls asking for me to write about stuff for them. I have now added these writings to my list for me to write this afternoon after my visit to B's Ma.

'Have you gotten any new writing tasks?' asked B as we walked up the drive towards his house.

'Yes, I have gotten three just this morning, I will be writing them once I leave here'

'That sounds like a fun yet busy afternoon'

'Indeed it will be haha' I laughed.

'Ma! We're here, where are you?' called Brendan into the house.

'In the living room!' his man called back.

'Ah, Emma! I haven't seen you in ages! How have you been? Has my boy been treating you well? Did you hear about my husband? Are you here out of pity?---' exclaimed Brendan's Ma.

'Ma! Give me some space. And slow down with the questions' interrupted B.

'I am well. Yes, he has. Yes, I did, it was terrible to hear. And I am not here out of pity. I bought you some homemade tea' I replied politely.

'Oh good, I'm glad you aren't here out of pity. I don't need pity. My husband made a mistake in leaving, he doesn't understand what he is missing'

'No, he certainly does not. Maybe one day he will realise that'

'I don't want him back'

'And I don't blame you. I wouldn't either'

'I'm glad you understand. Sorry, I'm not meaning to be rude. But I must let you go now, I have things that need to be done and I need to try some of your tea'

'Not rude at all, I have some telegrams to write. It was good seeing you, let me know if you need anything'

'Thank you, Emma'

After kissing B goodbye I made my way back to the house to write the telegrams.

***

Dear Mr. J Marin,

I have received a telegram. I understand your situation. I will write a small telegram back to you that you can then submit to your local paper. I am so happy that you reached out.

This is what I would like you to submit...please read it carefully, if your local newspaper has any objections to what I write then please send another telegram and I will change it up.

<u>*The devastating farmhouse fire*</u>

For those that are unaware, running and maintaining a farm is not an easy task, it takes more time and effort than a full-time job. Therefore anything that damages the farms, impacts the families that run and own it.

Today, I am writing about Mr. J Marin's farming disaster that left the family in shards.

On the 19th of October, Mr. J Marin and his family went out for supper to celebrate his daughter's birthday, when suddenly they got a telephone call saying that their farm was on fire. So, like everyone, the family rushed back home to help put the fire out. However, when they finally made it back, they were left with a shocking discovery!

Their whole farmhouse is nothing but a pile of ash and burnt wood. Their crop fields burnt. Gone. While bushfires happen regularly, farmhouse fires do not.

The firefighters fought hard to control the fire when they first arrived on the scene and the fire was put out within 30 minutes, after later inspection, the fire was said to be caused by a fault in the house fueling system due to a manufacturing issue that the company had issues with early this year, the company representatives told Mr. J Marin that the manufacturing issue doesn't affect his house and that they won't go and check it out.

Mr. J Marin has begun to sue the company for endangering his family, destroying his property, and neglecting their responsibilities. While this sounds like a great idea, the company won! AND they owe NOTHING to Mr. J Marin and his family!

A family left with nothing, a company unlawfully winning. I know our government and our law systems aren't always perfect, but Mr. J Marin and his family have now been left with nothing to call home, no food, no clothes, not even a job. If this is our government's way of being fair, I am less than impressed.

I am sending prayers out to Mr. J Marin and his family,

I cannot fathom why this happened to you, but it shouldn't happen again.

Written by:

Emma Hicks

***

One down, two to go... I thought before I started my second telegram.

Dear Mrs. E Harris,

I have received your telegram. I am so happy that you chose me to write it for you. I hope your novel is a best seller once published. Here is what I have to say about your written works, which I have seen around and have loved.

For those that may not know, Mrs. E Harris (Elizabeth Harris), (Pen name, Edward Harris), is a small town romance author, she has written three works so far, pending the release of no. 4. I am so excited to read it! Please be aware that Mrs. E Harris was forced to take on a male pen name to be able to submit her novels to publishers, if she used 'Elizabeth Harris', they would reject her instantly.

For those that may not know who I am, my name is Emma Hicks, I live in Kingship Valley, New South Wales with my sister, Maybelle, and my parents. I am a writer myself, I write for newspapers, companies, individuals needing advice or support, and myself. I am currently working on my own debut novel, titled Princess Julieanne.

Writing is my life, I don't know what I would do or who I would be without it. I grew up reading Jane Austen, the Bronte sisters, and lastly, Sylvia Plath. All of these authors have changed my views on the world, and have opened my eyes to accepting people and new experiences. Like many young writers, I have gone through many challenges when it comes to writing the best notes, stories, and articles. I am sure Mrs. E Harris would agree.

Mrs. E Harris has changed people's views on small country towns, she makes people want to visit them. While I am living in a small town, reading about other people's experiences always makes me consider everything that happens in my own life. While I cannot say that you are destined to find romantic love in a small town, I can say that you would find that the love of the community is enough, and the care that everyone has for one another is nothing like what you would find in the city.

I do hope that you all will enjoy reading this and reading Mrs. E Harris's work, I know I will.

Thank you Mrs. E Harris for the opportunity to write in your novel! I am honoured!

Best wishes,

Emma Hicks

***

After I had finished eating supper and cleaning up, I set to work on my last telegram of the day...

Dear Mr. L Hart,

I hope this telegram finds you well, I am glad you reached out looking for my advice.

My best advice for you is to never give up, keep drafting and editing your novels, and then approach a publisher and find out what they are looking for to see if your work fits their criteria. Most well known authors have approached many different publishers and edited their works over 5 times, or more!

If you are worried about the thoughts on a certain aspect of your writing, or a certain sentence then you can always change it up. Don't be afraid to put your name out there. Without having the courage to publish your work you will never get published. You have already done so much more than most! Completing a manuscript is huge! So many writers don't even do that, they lose inspiration or become bored with the storyline causing them to give up and move on to the next best writing.

You will never know unless you try!

I believe that everyone is an artist. Writers, drawers, painters, winemakers, seamstresses, clay sculptures, and lastly jewellery crafters. Everyone has a place in this world, everyone has a purpose. It is hard to find out what your purpose is without trying new things, without taking risks. I believe that your purpose is to let the world read your works, whether it is poetry, history, fiction, or nonfiction. Everyone has a place. Don't let anyone ever tell you differently.

Best of luck to you! You got this!

Best wishes,

Emma Hicks

Now, I just need to take this out and put it in my mailbox ready for Jerry to collect and send off. I hope they enjoy reading and that they feel inspired. I thought to myself as I headed to the mailbox.

CHAPTER FIVE

I began the next day with a pleasant surprise at my front door, a bunch of flowers from Brendan, with a note saying;

Dearest Em,

I love you forever and always. Never forget that. I don't know what I'd do without you, you are my life. My shooting star. My everything.

Love,

B

Smiling, I took my flowers to the kitchen and placed them in a vase.

These are beautiful. I thought. *I need to call him and thank him.* I continued to think as I made my way to the telephone.

Ring...ring...ring...

'Hello?' asked a sleepy voice on the other end of the telephone.

'Good morning, B' I replied.

'Em...I am guessing you got the flowers I sent you?'

'I did, they are beautiful thank you!'

'Not as beautiful as you'

'The note was sweet'

'I'm glad you like it. It took all of my brain power' Brendan's laugh echoed through the line causing me to smile.

'I love you, B'

'I love you the most, Em. But I am guessing you would need to go soon given the fact that these telephone calls never last long before they cut out'

'Yes, I do. And I also need to call the newspaper, find out if there are any new stories'

'That sounds like fun, I wish I could stop by today. But unfortunately, I need to work haha'

'I'll see you soon,' I concluded before hanging up the telephone.

He's the best. I thought as I lit the fire. Warming up the place is always my first priority.

Now, time to write more on Princess Julieanne...

***

'Phillips, have you seen my hair-brush?' asked Julieanne.

'Ah, yes! I moved it to the vanity, then you will always know where to find it' replied King Phillips.

'Thank you, I do tend to leave it around places, especially when I am in a hurry'

'You know, we do have hair stylists and makeup artist on hand, so you won't need to do your own'

'I am aware, but I like doing my own things. Especially when I am not required to go anywhere. But since they need the money to supply for their families I do tend to ask them to help me, even if I don't need them to'

'That is very nice of you, Darling'

'I do try'

'No wonder the people love you so much…'

'They love their King just as much, if not more'

'Doubtful, you are the best Queen anyone can ever ask for!'

'Agree to disagree. Now, my Father has asked me to meet him to go over some plans for ruling the entire kingdom, how exciting!'

'Have fun, let me know what you guys decide on. I have some errands to run and some papers that need signatures so I might not see you for a while. Don't worry Julieanne. Everything is going to work out. I know you didn't exactly want to marry for status, but I do know that you love me to some extent. And I know that I am lucky to have you by my side, I wouldn't want to rule without you'

'Thank you, Phillips,' I replied before leaving to go and meet with my Father.

He has a point, I never wanted to marry for status. But he also knows that I do love him, and I probably would have wanted to marry him if it wasn't forced by our parents. I do love ruling though, and I love my people. I guess it isn't all that bad. And the people do love me. But I now have a higher standard to keep up with, the Former Queen, before her passing was one of the best ever known, she was strong, kind, bold, and fearless but also caring. She would run charities for the poor, go down, and spend time with the people. She was down to earth, she never took anything she had for granted. Everyone loved her, as did I. However, she, unfortunately, died when giving birth to her second child, a baby girl. Sadly, neither she nor the baby survived. Leaving the kingdom in mourning and heartache, especially the Former King. Enough that the following week he put in the retirement announcement that King Phillips was to take his place on the throne earlier than expected, giving the kingdom some hope of changing and growing. Since he has always had the support of the people, becoming king felt right to him, something he was born to do, something he wanted. He is living his dream life…

***

Ring...ring...ring...

Darn, does that telephone ever stop ringing? I asked myself.

'Hello?' I answered.

'Hello, Emma. It's Edwardson. I can't talk for long, I just wanted to say that your article has just been published. I have been getting telephone calls all morning saying how great it reads and how much they want to see more of your writing. You surely made an impact, like always. The article was amazing. I have been told that Mr. Whitington will be sending you a telegram once again. I have sent over another paper with your next writing jobs, please continue writing, never stop. I must be getting going now, best of luck'

'Thank you, Edwardson,' I replied before hanging up.

Oh, Ma, Pa, and Maybelle should be arriving home today. I thought to myself as I went to get and answer the front door, the runner boy was quick today.

'Hello, Emma. This is from Edwardson, enjoy'

'Thank you, did he say anything else about it?'

'Nope, he was in a hurry this morning and had a meeting. All he said was to give it to you'

'No worries, thank you. Have a great day'

Now like every other day that I receive items from the runner boy, the first thing I always do is clean off my writing desk, read the notes and requirements, and set off to work.

Dear Emma,

Thank you for taking the time out of your busy day to write this for me.

I am an old friend of Edwardson, he has mentioned to me that you are the best writer that he has ever known, so with that, in mind, I am expecting an amazing article about my business.

I am the founder of Harvey and Co. We are a children's fashion line, we create clothing for children of all ages.

In the coming weeks we will be having a show, this is to show us our new products that are coming out. And since all of our clothes are made one-by-one it takes a while to get all of the stores together. The event will take place in Blacktown, New South Wales. On the 23rd of August.

I would like you to write a small article about my business, to promote my business and to get people to want to go to our next fashion show.

I hope this telegram finds you well,

All the best,

Mr. P Harvy

Perfect, a fashion show article. Just want what I need. I thought as I set to work to write the best fashion article.

***

Harvey and Co

The founder of Harvey and Co, Mr.P Harvy has recently brought a fashion show to my attention, on the 23rd of August in Blacktown. While I personally am unable to attend, I will be sad to miss such an event.

For those who are unaware, Harvey and Co. is a children's clothing brand. They support children from both city lifestyles and small town lifestyles. The fashion range is incredible and the prices are great, you can buy both cheap clothing or higher end. This allows families from all walks of life to buy their clothing. The brand is sustainable and environmentally friendly, all of its products are handmade and, therefore, are in limited stock.

I have owned their products in the past, and I absolutely loved them. I am yet to buy new clothing from them as I am currently too large for their size, however, I am thinking about putting an order in for my younger sister. This brand is incredible and does not get the attention that it deserves.

Go to the show! Buy their clothes! Have a good time!

Written by,

Emma Hicks

***

'Honey, are you home?' called Ma from the front door.

'Ma! Your home!' I cried as I ran to greet them by the front door.

'Yes...we are,' she replied with a smile.

'Hello, Darling" greets Pa as Maybelle and himself make it to the door.

'How was it?' I asked as I excitedly made my way to the kitchen to put the kettle on. Ma and Pa always loved coffee when they arrived home from long trips.

'It was amazing, the beaches are amazing!' replied Maybelle excitedly and she ran over to me and wrapped her arms around me.

'I bet! I've got the kettle boiling for your coffee. Maybelle, did you want some tea?' I asked.

'Oh yes, please! I've missed your tea!' she replied while grabbing out the glassware.

'So, Emma. What have you been up to?' asked Pa.

'I've just finished writing another article for the paper. I submitted one for Kahibi last week which was very successful. I've sent out a telegram to both Grandmother and Uncle Mick, waiting to hear back from them both. I replied to a couple of telegrams from people looking for advice, and an author reached out and wanted me to write a small paragraph about myself for her next book!'

'Which author?' asked Ma curiously.

'Elizabeth Harris, well, technically Edward Harris. If you want her pen name that is'

'Ah yes, I believe you own one of her books, correct? Didn't you also write a book review in the papers for her book?'

'Yes, to both. I think that is one of the reasons that she reaches out, to begin with'

'Or it could just be that she has read your work and saw how talented you are' suggested Pa.

'Maybe' I remarked.

'How's your book?' asked Maybelle.

'It is progressing very well, I think. Maybe one day I'll finish it and publish it'

'I am sure so many people would be keen to read it, I know I am. Especially since you won't tell anyone about it. Well, except Maybelle but she won't tell us about it' complained Ma.

'Yes, well it needs to be a surprise for you and Pa. Coffee is ready' I say as I hand their mugs over to them. 'I've already got the fire burning, so now all you guys need to relax! Read a book or something!' I continued.

Once Ma, Pa, and Maybelle were seated around the fireplace, I informed them that I needed to write another telegram and that I would be back out once it was finished.

***

Dear Miss. L Norton,

Thank you so much for your telegram! I am so glad that you and the family are doing well!

I hear that your business is booming with new customers this season! I mean your dresses are always amazingly designed and look amazing on you! Have you found any more models for your next launch yet? I will continue to support your business from afar. I am sure I will get the chance to write again for the fashion section of the paper, especially since yours will be featured in this July's edition. And your winter dresses always look so warm!

Please send me a telegram if there is anything I can do to help support you more!

How are your dogs going? Oh, and I hear that you are re-modeling your house! I bet that is so exciting! I look forward to seeing it! Send me some photos once it is finished too! I can't wait to see it!

I'm planning on looking into saving up some money for the summer so I can buy one of your amazing summer dresses! I just love them so much! They are so cute!

I look forward to seeing you!

Love you lots,

From your bestie,

Emma

***

Knock...knock...knock...

'I've got it' announced Ma as she got up and answered the door. 'Ah! Brendan! Come in' Ma continued.

'Emma! Brendan's here!'

'I'm coming Ma!' I called back.

'Thank you, Mrs Hicks. How was your trip?' I could hear Brendan ask Ma as I walked into the hallway. Greeting Brendan with a smile.

'It was amazing, Brendan. Are you guys going out somewhere?' she asked quizzically.

'That depends on Em...' Brendan answered.

'Where would we go?' I questioned. Once Ma had left us relatively alone. But we are always aware that everything echoes through this house.

'I was thinking of the sunflower fields?'

'In the middle of winter? It's freezing outside'

'It's not that bad once you start moving around, it's only cold if you stay still and don't do anything...come on! Let go and have some fun!' he pleaded.

'Fine, but I must not be out late, they have only just arrived home. So, I do happen to want to spend some time with them'

'And you will have most of the night to do that' he remarked.

'Fine...bye Ma, Pa and Maybelle! I'll be home soon!' I called.

***

'So, why did you choose to go out tonight? I told you my family was returning home today' I complained.

'I know that hence the reason I stole you tonight. You never say no to coming out when your Ma is home since otherwise she scolds you for being antisocial'

'Well played...'

'I know it was. But in my defense, I never see you anymore, Em. And I know you are busy with your job and writing telegrams and of course your book. But even so...'

'I know, B. I'm sorry about that. I will try to make more time for you, deal?'

'I would love that'

'So please don't tell me you dragged me out of my warm house for this conversation?'

'What! No, absolutely not. Haha,' his laugh broke the serene silence of the night, pure, loving, and blissful to hear.

'Good!' I laughed back.

'Right, Em. Now that we have that out of the way, what would you like to do?'

'So you didn't plan anything?' I asked as I grabbed hold of his hand and continued to walk alongside him down the cold dirt road.

Why did he want to do this in winter? I thought as I walked alongside B.

'I have some ideas...'

'Well then, let's hear them!' I announced.

'Alright, alright! Patience!'

'Something I don't have!'

'Ok, so idea one, we go and lay in the fields and look at the stars. Idea two, we go for a walk to the heated pond. And that's it'

'They both sound like fun, but if we went to the heated pond, then we'd go into it. Which is fine except when we have to get out we will be frozen. So, to conclude, looking up at the stars sounds relaxing, as long as we don't come across any snakes that is' I replied.

'Star gazing it is!' he says before running off.

'Hey! Wait for me!' I called into the calm night.

Cold, blissful, peaceful winter nights, are the best nights according to Ma. She loves winter, although it doesn't snow here, so it isn't as cold as in some places, I guess we have a nice winter here. Maybe...

CHAPTER SIX

I have always wondered what it would be like in the future, will there be flying cars? Will the cars be faster? Will our beautiful steam trains still be running? While these questions often float to the front of my mind, I always continue to think of more questions. I am, of course, well aware that more of these questions won't be able to be answered, at least I can leave it all up to my imagination, therefore, I cannot be disappointed.

I am often left wondering if writing will become more popular if people from all parts of the world can access and read people's works. Will telegrams still be a thing? Will the telephone service be able to reach outside of one town?

Will there be a way for people to access newspapers, and written works easier without having to wait?

'Emma?!?' called Ma from the kitchen.

'Coming Ma,' I called back.

Once I quickly changed my clothing and put it away, I made my way to the kitchen. The kitchen was filled with fresh foods, drinks, and tea making supplies. The smell of fresh coffee filled the cold winter air.

'Ah, there you are darling! I have just gotten back from the markets. I got you some more tea supplies, there is mail for you also. I have received numerous requests for your teas while I was at the market, they are becoming high in demand. Therefore, you need to make more and sell. I have set the mail on the counter' Ma continued while she quickly pointed to the countertop behind me.

'Thanks, Ma. I will make the teas and set them out to dry shortly'

'That would be lovely, especially when we are also running out ourselves'

I gathered up the mail and headed back towards my room to open them. I hope that there will be another article in it somewhere that I will be able to write today. I enjoyed writing articles.

The first telegram is from one of the townsfolk;

Emma, I would like some more tea please, Kara.

Short and simple, Kara always is. She likes getting straight to the point.

The second one was from Mr. A Whitington;

Dear Emma,

So sorry for the delayed response to your previous telegram! I have been crazy busy replying to telegrams and telephone calls about the article that you wrote about Kahibi!

I am very, very thankful for the article! You have made quite an impact! Everyone loved it, including myself!

I definitely made the right choice in asking you to write it for me, I can now see why so many people go to you for guidance and for you to write things for them! Your writing is undoubtedly the best Kingship Valley has ever had! All of the surrounding towns are lucky to have you in reach! The wider world doesn't understand what they are missing out on!

I understand that you have written articles through telegrams for people to take to their local newspapers, that is a great way to get your name out there! Continue to do that and you will have more and more telegrams coming your way!

Best of luck to you and thank you! I am looking forward to working with you in the future, Kahibi needs someone as passionate as you writing about it.

Yours thankfully,

Mr. A Whitington

His telegrams are always delightful to read. I thought as I tried to figure out how to reply.

Dear Mr. A Whitington,

Thank you for your telegram! It was my honour to write to you on behalf of Kahibi!

Your town deserves to be recognised!

I am glad you enjoyed reading the article. To be honest, I was a little worried that you wouldn't like it. Sometimes my writing upsets readers, as I always speak the truth. Some people don't like that.

I am looking forward to and excited to be working alongside you on future articles! Please reach out if there is anything I can do to help you!

Best wishes,

Emma Hicks

*Right, now that is out of the way. I still have one more to open...*I thought.

Dear Emma,

I have just received a new writing task for you, sorry I couldn't call. I have gone out of town, I hope this telegram finds you well.

I have attached another telegram with your instructions and the key focus points for the article.

I believe you are going to love writing about this one!

Best regards,

Edwardson

I pulled out the second paper that read,

Instructions:

- *Young writers need recognition*

- *People's works are being taken for granted or sold/stolen to make someone else look like the writer.*

- *Scammers twist people's words, making them a villain.*

Include what you wish, Emma. But make sure you acknowledge how wrong this all is.

-Edwardson.

That's horrible! I will write this tonight. Firstly, I need to make some tea. I thought in horror of this article and what it means for young novelists globally.

***

I began spooning the tea leaves into the jars and bags ready for them to be delivered to the townsfolk.

'Emma? Have you finished the tea yet?' asked Pa.

'Yes, Pa! I am just packing them, I have orders that I am putting together, I have left our lot on the counter near the coffee' I called back.

'Wonderful'

As I packed up the tea I couldn't help but wonder what it would be like to own my own tea company, in a city where there would be lots of people to buy my tea, it would be so much fun.

'Emma, darling. I will be heading into town shortly, I will deliver the tea for you. I am sure you have writing tasks to complete. Correct?'

'Yes, Ma. I always do. I have to write about scammers stealing young novelists' work in order to gain recognition and profit from them'

'Oh, that's horrible! Why would they do such a thing, it's wrong'

'It is what some people do to make money'

'Clearly, now go and write it! It is not going to write itself, now is it?'

'No, of course not' I replied before making my way back to my room to begin writing about the scandalous writing disaster.

***

The Scandalous Writing Disaster

It has come to my attention that young novelists' works are getting stolen and used to make a profit through someone else. I have no idea what gives people rights or the willpower to do something so appallingly wrong!

There are so many young novelists out there who are looking for a way to let their voices be heard through their writing, whether it is through articles, promotions, or even novels.

Nobody's work should EVER be taken from them under any circumstances. It is wrong and cruel. If you didn't take the time and effort into writing something then you should not be getting the recognition and profit from it.

It is reported that 11 hundred novelists have had their works stolen and resold in the past year, this is unacceptable. When is our government going to step in and stop this from happening?

I myself, am classified as a young novelist, I would be heartbroken if someone stole my works for resale purposes. It's wrong and I cannot begin to justify how disgusted I am that this is happening to so many individuals.

If this is something that has happened to you, please send me a telegram.

I have recently received a telegram asking for writing advice, this is something I love to do, but for me to gain an understanding of the genre and the topics of the work the author/s needs to share information with me, I cannot begin to fathom the thought of people reaching out to one another for writing help and the next thing you know is that your works/concepts are being sold before you even get the chance to release it yourself.

To all of the young novelists out there, don't give up. Keep on re-porting when this happens. Send me a telegram, I'd be happy to write an-

other article addressing this inhuman
insult to writers globally.

Our government needs to step in and
put a stop to this disgraceful behaviour! It's appalling that they
haven't already done this!

People deserve their voice to be
heard, do not allow people to take
that right away from them.

Written by:

Emma Hicks

                    ***

Knock...knock...knock...

'Emma! Jerry's here!' called Ma from the front door.

'Coming Ma!' I called back.

Quickly, I gathered my telegrams and hurried down the stairs.

'Hello, Jerry. Here are the telegrams that I need posted' I announced as I arrived at the foot of the door.

''Ello, Emma. Thanks. I shall 'ave 'em off to post this 'arvo' he replied as he took them from my hand.

'That would be amazing, Jerry. Thank you'

'You welcome, Emma. I must be off, I 'ave some more errands to run this 'arvo'

'Have a good afternoon'

''ave yourself a break, Emma' he replied before turning away.

Jerry is always a pleasure, he lightens up everyone's day by saying hello. I thought to myself as I headed towards the kitchen to make some tea.

'Emma! Can you make me one too, please?' asked Maybelle.

'Sure, does anyone else want one?' I called back.

'Yes, please' Ma and Pa replied in unison.

Every time someone makes tea or coffee in this house, someone else wants one too. I guess we all love tea and coffee.

The kettle always takes forever to boil, especially since we have an older gas stove. They released an upgrade a couple of months back but we don't have the money for it. We save our money for more important things such as food, water, clothing, our house, and lastly our education. We have always spent our money on things that we need, nothing besides that. Unless Maybelle or myself use our own money for things.

As I made my family some tea I couldn't help but wonder if I would be so lucky to have such an amazing family in another time, or if I would be living a completely different life with a different family. I quite often wondered this, wondered what it would be like living in a busy city with a lot of money to spend, but I also found myself wondering if I would want any of that and if I did have it all would I want to live the life I currently had? Whilst I know that these questions will never be answered, I liked hoping. I liked dreaming and wishing. Even though some of my dreams and wishes will never come true.

Once the teas were finished, I headed towards my family, all sitting near the fireplace, ambers glowing against their faces. Illuminating them like angels.

'Ah thank you, Emma' thanks Ma as she grabs her tea from the carrying plate.

After I handed everyone their tea, I headed back to the kitchen and placed the carry plate near the kettle, before reaching for my cup and returning to the living room.

'Do you have any jobs tomorrow, Emma?' asked Pa.

'Currently, no. But I will know more in the morning' I replied.

'I wish they gave you more notice...'

'Yes, Ma. They try to. But most of the time the stories that are given to the newspaper are given the night before, they need to be reviewed before handing it out to the writers, otherwise we will end up with false things in the paper, or non-relevant information'

'Why can't people get it to the newspaper sooner then?' asked Maybelle.

'Because it takes time for the victims or people asking for it to be written to write up the summary and it takes a while for it to come through the telegram. And most stories are outside of the reach of the telephones, therefore, people cannot contact the newspaper sooner'

'Makes a little sense, I guess,' replied Maybelle.

'They should come up with a quicker way for it to get to the writers' commented Pa.

'True, but I don't mind waiting–'

'But you shouldn't have to,' interrupted Ma.

'Right, well I best be off to bed. Good night' I replied as I rose and headed for my bedroom.

'Good night, Emma' they all said in unison.

I might just quickly write some more on my story. I thought.

***

'Father! Why is the Kingdom planning a birthday celebration? I don't like having big things on my birthday, you know that. And so do the people, they haven't done it before' asked Queen Julieanne.

'True, they haven't. But before you weren't their Queen, now you are.

Therefore, it is tradition to throw a party on the Queen's birthday, same as the King' he replied.

'But I never asked for one'

'You didn't need to'

'But it's for my birthday, shouldn't I have a say?'

'Not when it comes to this Kingdom's traditions. The people follow the traditions, to get the tradition to change you would need to hold a meeting with King Phillips, the Former King, the official speaker on behalf of the people, yourself, and of course with me. It would then be put to a vote, if you do win and the tradition is deemed non-important, then it would depend on whether the people continue to do it or not. We may make the choices that impact them, but we cannot force them to stop. I'll leave the choice up to you, Julieanne'

'So even if I did hold this meeting the people still would celebrate it anyway?'

'Yes, most likely'

'Then what would be the point of the meeting?'

'That depends on how much you want the tradition to end, eventually, it will'

'Right…'

'Don't change thousands of years of traditions because you don't like birthdays. Every Queen and King after you will have to accept that you broke tradition and that you are the reason they don't get to celebrate their birthdays with the people'

'Wow, one way to make me feel guilty without me even doing it yet'

'That is the point, think about all the consequences before you make a choice. As Queen you will need to make many choices that you will not like, nor will you morally agree with'

'I already know that'

'Yes, but trust me, Julieanne. The choices that you have made so far are nothing to the ones you will need to make'

'I watched the Former Queen for years, I've been there when she made tough choices. I already know and understand some of the choices that will be made. Besides that the Former Queen was teaching me tips for becoming the best possible Queen, therefore, I already know some of what to expect'

'Yes, I am aware. You and the Former Queen kept sneaking out of the guards' protection and she was teaching you the ways to become Queen. But it is different watching and learning than what it is becoming Queen'

```
'True, I guess there is only one real
way to find out'
```

***

Once I was at peace with what I had written that night I got ready for bed, excited for a blissful, dream filled slumber...

CHAPTER SEVEN

There is nothing better than feeling the warm sun against my cold cheeks on bitter cold winter mornings. Feeling the heavenly sensation warming the room. It is one of the very many reasons I love the sun. Only, it was pouring down, the rain coming down hard, relentlessly.

An eerie silence filled the house that morning. The silence occupied a gut wrenching heartache. The silence of loss, death, and sorrow.

I arose this morning from a knock at the door, Ma was the first one to answer the door. I normally loved mornings, but this morning was different. Much, much different.

There is nothing worse than hearing your Ma cry out in despair and heartbreak. It's heartbreaking to hear, this of course made me jump straight out of bed and rush to where Ma was on her knees crying. The pageboy- or rather a man- was standing there, looking so sorry.

I helped Ma out to the lounge room, before returning to the door.

'Are you Emma?' asked the pageboy.

'Yes...' I replied, uneasy about the whole situation.

'There was an accident at the mines...I'm sorry, your Pa didn't make it out. He is a brave man, he saved 7 lives before the mine completely collapsed'

I felt as if I had just been punched in the gut and my heart was ripped out.

'Th...thank...yo..u' she stumbled.

'If there is anything you need please let me or the mayor know' he replied before turning away, leaving me standing shocked in the doorway.

'Emma? What's going on?' asked Maybelle from behind her.

Oh no! How am I supposed to tell her? I thought in panic.

'Girls...' called Ma silently, barely audible over the pounding, relentless rain.

'Coming Ma!' replied Maybelle.

'Emma...I am sure you are aware of what has happened to your Pa...' Ma whispered, barely speaking at all.

'Y...yes' I stumbled out.

'Would you care to grab us some tea?' Ma asked.

'Of course,' I replied.

When I was in the kitchen she could hear Ma stumbling out what had happened at the mines, sobbing after every second word. Followed by Maybelle's earth shattering scream.

The family had always dreaded this happening...but they didn't expect it to be today. Today was Maybelle's 14th birthday.

Now Maybelle will remember her 14th as the day she lost her Pa...

The family tried to reason with Pa that the mines were too dangerous, but he insisted that they needed the money. It was the best paying job in the area, but it also came with the most risks.

'Emma?' called Ma.

Once I regained myself, I headed to where Maybelle and Ma sat in the living room. I had to be brave for them. I just had to...

'Is the tea ready?' asked Maybelle.

'Yes, I'll bring it in,' I replied.

Once I returned, tea in hand, I sat down next to Maybelle and held her until her sobs became softer, until she fell asleep. Ma was watching the fire, off in her own world.

'She's finally calmed down, even to fall asleep anyway' I informed Ma as I untangled myself and walked over to Ma, sitting down and holding her.

I have no idea how long we sat there, arm in arm, watching the flames dance around each other.

If we were doing this at any other time then it would be wonderful, relaxing by the fire with the ones I love watching flames dance like ballerinas. It would be magical.

But today, the flames of the fire, the warmth, aren't the same. It reminds me of destruction, death, grief, and longing. This saddens me, I love fires and the way the flames dance around each other, loss makes everything appear different, new, and horrible.

***

The following morning, I called the newspaper and informed them that I would be taking a couple of days off to mourn the loss of Pa. I insisted with Ma that I would continue to make and sell my teas so that they would receive some sort of income.

Maybelle was affected the worst by the loss of Pa, she wasn't that close to him, but she felt drawn to him. Like she knew him inside and out. Pa has always encouraged me to go after my dreams, this is the same with Maybelle. However, Pa loved my writing and was the first and biggest supporter of it. He was the one who approached the newspaper on my behalf. He made me become the person I am today. Maybelle spent little time with Pa, but Pa had a personality where if you meet him once you will forever be touched by him, nobody ever had or could hate him, everyone in town loved him.

Ring...ring...

'I'll get it' I called as I headed downstairs.

'Hello?' I answered.

'Ah, Em. How are you and the family holding up?' asked Brendan.

'Hey, B. Mum and Maybelle are grief struck, they won't leave their rooms or eat anything'

'Sounds tough'

'Yeah...'

'Did you want me to come over?'

'If you want,' she replied. 'But I have to go, as the telephone will be cut out soon,' I continued.

'Ok, I might come over'

'Ok, I'll see you shortly, B'

'Bye, Em' Brendan concluded.

I always feel relieved after hearing Brendan's voice. I feel calmer. He always had this effect on me, no matter what the circumstances were.

The house had an eerie silence about it and has since Pa's untimely death. The house will never be the same again, this makes me sad. I loved my Pa dearly and never expected nor wanted this to happen to him of all people, but he died nobly. That has to count for something...right?

I quite often found myself wandering the house looking at pictures of the family, of Pa. Wishing he was with me now and not taken away. I often thought this way when

I was alone, without having to worry about Maybelle and Ma. The last two days have been hell for the family, and now they need to arrange the burial. The townsfolk have delivered flowers, cakes, pies, and small gifts or money to help with the burial costs and living costs. We thank everyone for their assistance, Ma insists that we 'don't need charity', I for one think it is very sweet of the town to help us, and all of the other families impacted. Those that my Pa saved were extra thankful, for those that also lost their Pa, brother, grandfather, or uncle have also thanked us or sent condolences. I have been sending telegrams out to all of the families that were impacted by this nightmare of a disaster.

'Emma?' called Brendan.

'Come in!' I called back.

When Brendan finally appeared in view, I jumped into his arms. I missed him dearly and was very thankful that he did not work in the mines.

'I don't know what I would do if I'd lost you in the mines too, never work there' I cried.

'I have no intentions of it, Em. So you have nothing to worry about

'Good...' I replied, finally able to recover my composure.

God, how I hated crying...

'I'm going to go and send my regards to Mrs. Hicks' announced Brendan.

'Ok, I'll wait near the fireplace' I replied.

While I paced in front of the fireplace I couldn't help but wonder what Ben was doing, he left for the city late last night. He left in a hurry. His new employer told him to come in as soon as possible, therefore, Ben was unable to say goodbye before he left. He is probably nearing the city by now, given that the day is almost over.

Ben and I have been together since we were kids, it is going to be hard without him present in my life. I'm going to miss him dreadfully.

Finally, I resigned to sitting in front of the fire, Brendan was taking his time with Ma and Maybelle. Nothing out of the ordinary there. But given the circumstances, I expected him to stay with them for a while, he wants to make sure they are ok as much as I do. Generally, if this was any other circumstance I would be upset that he is spending more time with them than me, but I'm not.

Maybe, I should write Ben a telegram? By the time he arrives at the city and is settled, the telegram won't take long to get to him after that point. It would be perfect timing. But what would I write? I thought to myself.

'Everything ok?' asked Brendan as he gracefully entered the remorseful room.

'Um, yeah...just thinking'

'About...?' he prodded.

'Everything'

Sighing, Brendan took a seat next to me. I ditched the formalities and sat on the floor rather than the armchairs. Once we were both settled in front of the fire, my head on his shoulder, his arm wrapped around my waist, providing me comfort. It would be the perfect picture.

'You know it isn't your fault, right?' announced B.

'Yeah, I guess,' I sighed.

'You couldn't have done anything differently to prevent this from happening'

'I could have convinced Pa to leave the mines...'

'Yes, but if you did do that, more people would have died, more families losing their loved ones. As far as I and the rest of the town are concerned, your Pa died a hero, everyone is grateful for his bravery'

'I guess...'

As the sun sets on the horizon, Brendan and I watch the fire dwindle to ashes wondering what life will be like over the next couple of days...

CHAPTER EIGHT

'Emma, when do you return to work?' asked Maybelle.

'I am starting back up today, relax, I have been making soaps and teas for the townsfolk to supply us with some income. " I replied coolly. My voice lacks its usual empathy. The last few days have been exhausting, and we all need a break from each other. Thankfully, I have reading and writing that provides the escape that Ma and Maybelle are missing.

It has been over a week since Pa's abrupt departure from our lives, nothing seems to be taking away the heartache accompanied by the death of a loved one.

But I am now due to return to work, and I have fallen behind on replying to telegrams, even ones from family members. The family has fallen into sorrow over their loss, the funeral took place three days ago, followed by a group memorial to mourn the loss of the townsfolk. The whole town mourns the loss of their family and friends, some more than others. This has made Kingship Valley the most sorrowful place in NSW, this is more tragic than our little town can handle at once. This is the most tragic accident that Kingship Valley has ever had, which in turn means that I will be responsible for writing the newspaper article, something that I have been dreading since the accident occurred. Unfortunately, I am the only novelist qualified to write about this tragedy.

'Will you be writing about the accident today?' asked Ma as she wandered into the kitchen and stopped before the kettle, ready for her first coffee of the morning. The family has been going through more coffee and teas than they ever have in the past.

'Yes...I guess I will be'

'Good, it is better to get it over and done with...'

'I guess...I will also be replying to telegrams and writing other articles over the next couple of days, so I won't be making much tea. Thankfully, I completed all of our last orders' I replied.

'How do you make it?' inquired Maybelle.

'You cannot make it, Maybelle. You have school to return to'

'I can' prompted Ma.

'No, you also have to work. I will continue making the teas and the soaps in my spare time, the townsfolk can wait for their orders to be fulfilled, if they need it before a certain date then they can let me know, otherwise, I will make it when I can'

'The townsfolk will understand. They are all still grieving as well'

'Yes, I am aware. Maybelle you should be heading to school and Ma you need to shower and head to work. You have barely left the house since Pa's death. It will be good for you to get out again'

'I know...' she replied solemnly.

Once Ma and Maybelle had left the house, I set to work tidying the kitchen, bathroom, her room, Maybelle's and Ma's room as well as the dining room and lounge room. The family has been slack in their house maintenance since Pa's death, which is worrying, especially since Ma never has anything out of place.

***

*Right, time to get to work...*I thought once I finished my long list of tasks, now firstly, I need to write a telegram to Ben. He has sent me seven over the last couple of days.

Dearest Ben,

Sorry, I haven't replied to any of your telegrams. I am sure you are worried sick. I didn't feel up to writing.

I am sure you have heard the rumors floating around, yes there was a mining accident that killed 70 workers and yes my Pa was one of them.

I am told that Pa died a hero, he saved 30 people before the mines collapsed. I think that is meant to make us feel better but to be honest, it doesn't bring him back and it doesn't change anything. The families that were saved feel obliged to support and help my family, they feel as if it is their duty that we are looked after.

Kingship Valley is in full shambles, the town mayor is doing everything he can to support the townsfolk, but everyone is grieving so everyone is watching what they say and how they act around each other. It's like a depressed prison here at the moment. And nothing anyone says or does can change that.

Ma and Maybelle have been struggling a lot over the loss of Pa. Ma hasn't left her room, let alone the house. Maybelle hasn't left the house at all, mostly mopping in her room or in front of the fire.

Brendan has come over a couple of times to check on everyone, he even stayed the night a couple of times and Ma didn't stop him. Even the house has been messy, which as you know, Ma hates.

I have started up my soap and tea business again, which has been successful. Especially my 'Cheer Up' blends of tea and my 'Get Well Soon' blends. But even with the teas and the soaps, it still cannot take any of the grief and heartache that fills the town. Nothing can.

I am doing ok, as well as can be expected given the circumstances. I am due to write about the accident, this article will be featured in many newspapers throughout New South Wales, so you will receive it also.

I hope your new job is going well and that they are treating you well.

I wish you were here, I miss you so much.

Love,

Emma Hicks

One down, heaps to go. I thought to myself.

Dear Edwardson,

I hope this telegram finds you well, my understanding is that you have gone away for three days, and this telegram will find you before you return home. Please call me when you return.

I will be writing about the mining accident over the next couple of days, apologies for the delay. It will be ready for the next newspaper printing. I will get the company to send the article to local and national newspaper companies. This story deserves the attention of our country, not just our local community. This incident will be featured on the front page of every local newspaper. In terms of the national newspaper companies, I am unsure where they would place it within the paper, as it obviously isn't a main feature for them.

I will be sending in a draft to the editor, this way he can refine/edit it for me.

I look forward to your return.

Best wishes,

Emma Hicks

The national newspapers will be shocked at the discovery that such a story will be written by a young novelist, let alone a female one. Our world is horrid towards females, most don't even have many job options. They are to assume the roles of wife, mother, and maid. Nothing more, nothing less. Females who do not produce children are frowned upon. The females in our society who have jobs work as seamstresses, maids, and nannies, especially teachers. If you are lucky, then you would be given the job of a nurse or a midwife, granted, no matter what profession women go into they still don't receive the same amount of respect, privileges, or income as their male counterparts. You are even more segregated if you are of a different nationality or do not fit the stereotypical, idealised caucasian look of an upperclassman or ones that you find in the paper. Stereotypically, the male sex is more powerful and superior to their women counterparts. One day I hope that this will change, that women get paid the same as their male counterparts, that women get their own choice of career, that women can choose whether or not to have children and get married without being shunned or disowned by their community and families. Most importantly, I hope that women don't have to be controlled and commanded by others, especially males.

While I try to keep my views to myself every now and again they slip out in my writing, I believe that these things should be addressed. But I also know that the world I live in cannot handle the amount of chances, the lack of power some will feel, and the lack of control. I don't think some of our society would be able to handle that so therefore, they won't cooperate.

I have always had strong views on issues, whether they are political or small things that impact the community, I also understand that most of my views I need to keep to myself and not go public about due to the fact that it would ruin my writing career before it even kicked off, and given the fact that most of the writing community are males, and when a female enters a reporting position they are often segregated and left to write and report in women's sections of the newspaper, they were almost never given big events to write about. I have worked hard to get where I am and do not plan on giving up, I get paid less than my male counterparts, and I have to constantly compete with the males in the industry, not to mention societal views on my writing. While I have my town's respect and encouragement, the rest of the world isn't so forthcoming and nice about the whole affair.

Right...who next? Maybe I should start the article, and get it out of the way? I thought.

Mining accident that killed 70+ people

This terrible disaster took place in a small rural town in New South Wales, Australia. Kingship Valley is known for its friendly community, great support system, and agriculture.

Kingship Valley is a town built solely on the trust that people have with one another, the town wouldn't survive without it.

The mines were Kingship Valley and surrounding towns such as Kahibi's main source of power and fuel. The mines are currently under construction and will not be able to be operated on for the next couple of months if there is anything left saving.

The town is mourning the loss of loved ones and friends. 70+ lives were lost in the mines, that's 70+ loved ones who are grieving.

One man stood out from the rest, that saved 30 people before the mines collapsed, this man is known as Reginald Hicks.

Reginald Hicks was a proud man, father, husband, and friend to many. The loss of Mr R. Hicks will be felt for many, many years to come.

Mr R. Hicks will be going down in Kingship Valley's history books, as the man that saved 30 lives, in a mining collapse that should have killed them all.

The families that have their loved ones today, are extremely thankful and have been thanking Mr R. Hicks's family constantly.

While some families are still together, there are unfortunately some that have been torn apart, with sons lost, fathers, husbands, uncles, and grandparents. None of these people should have died, none of their families should be suffering. I send out my sincerest condolences for your loss…

This accident will never be forgotten by the people of Kingship Valley and the surrounding towns.

Written by:

Emma Hicks

I am so glad that it is done and dusted. I don't know what I'd do if I ever needed to write something like this about my home... I thought as I headed towards the kitchen to prepare for supper.

CHAPTER NINE

It is now the beginning of spring, the time of the year when plants and animals thrive in the warmer weather. It has now been 3 months since Pa's untimely demise, I miss him dreadfully every day. But like many have said before me, 'everything happens for a reason' and 'life goes on'. While both of these things may be true, they both make people feel sad, especially when the things that happen are tragic. On a day-to-day basis, so many people are suffering or grieving. And this is so unfair to many. But it is also a part of life, you cannot live without death following closely behind.

The biggest sacrifice people will make in their lifetime is death, but it is cherishable if they leave something behind. The most important things to leave behind are knowledge and love, the two things that keep this world going. Without these things, the world would be chaotic and wasted. But the fear of death and the unknown makes people want to make the best of their lives, they want to learn, grow, explore, and love. They want to live a life worth living. They have to share their knowledge with their children in order to keep their spirit alive once they pass and hope that the knowledge that they share with their children will continue to be passed down through generations to come.

While death is terrifying, it is also beautiful. Death is associated with a new life, being reborn. It allows the soul to move on, resting in eternal happiness. Happiness that people long for, they finally receive it.

'Emma?' called Brendan.

'Brendan? What are you doing here?' I asked.

'I'm coming to see you obviously, how are you?'

'Tired and stressed'

'Have you still been receiving telegrams of hatred towards you for being a writer and publishing an article?'

'Yes, the rest of Australia doesn't want female writers, especially on the front page of the national newspapers'

'That must be hard'

'Yes, this is why I try to stay within our town, as soon as my writing goes national, I begin to receive these telegrams and our newspaper is also receiving them. Shedding poor light on them as well. Bad publicity can be the end of my career and the end of our newspaper'

'What are they going to do about it?'

'Honestly, I'm not too sure...'

'Will they continue to let you write?'

'I hope so, but until the world has calmed down, I won't be writing at nationally recognised levels, just locally. One day, I hope to change societal views on female novelists, but for now, I will need to be patient. There aren't enough female novelists that are vocal enough to stand up for their beliefs and for what is right'

'I guess, I hope you receive national recognition for your writing, or even international. Either way, you are still a star around here, one that the world won't be able to ignore or extinguish'

'Thanks, B. I do believe that if enough people voice their concerns and disbelief about the lack of opportunities in the world and the government system, then they wouldn't be able to ignore it'

'I think so too'

'Unfortunately, that won't be today, or even in my time. But I do hope it happens in the future, I think it would make the world a much better place'

'What's your plans today?' asked B.

'I need to write a telegram to Gran, she sent us one, but I am yet to reply. And the newspaper has given me a small writing gig, but they haven't given me much lately as they don't want to ignite the press into giving our town more grief over having a female novelist'

'Fair enough, I guess that makes sense...we don't want our town getting a bad reputation, not that I think you would make that happen. But the world can be a cruel place'

'Indeed it can be'

'How's your book going too?'

'It's getting there, about halfway through, I will be writing some more on it today'

'That's a great idea, it is going to be amazing once it is finished'

'Even once I finish it, I won't be able to find someone willing to release my work, as it would be a nationally recognised book, and as we know, people don't like a female novelist. And that is only over one article clipping from the newspaper'

'Have you considered printing your book under a male name?'

'And lose the use of my name being associated with it? Absolutely not. If I am going to go through all of the trouble of writing it and publishing it then I am going to use my name, proudly'

'I have heard that there is a couple of different female novelists using male names for publication purposes'

'Yes, but I am not those other people'

'Yes, definitely not. Well, I best be getting going, I have some errands to run for Ma'

'Ok, how is your Ma going?'

'She is better now, I think the initial shock of him leaving has passed'

'Well, that's good,' I replied as he made his way to the front door.

Now that he is gone, I can finally write more on my story...

***

Oh, how Julieanne hated parties, she was expected to dance. She hates dancing. She is expected to talk to random people from other kingdoms, another thing she doesn't like to do.

But I guess that is another downfall of being the Queen.

'Your Highness?'

'Yes, Roseanne?' I replied.

'I have been asked to come and assist you in packing…' she replied, quietly.

'I don't need help, but thank you'

'Yes, he said you'd say that. But I have been ordered to stay with you…so please give me something to do so I don't feel useless'

'Who told you to come up here?'

'Um…'

'Roseanne?'

'Your father…'

'I am your Queen, which means I override my father's authority'

'Yes, I understand that… but your father is also still a powerful man, he is best friends with the former king, therefore, I can still get into trouble for not following his instruction'

'Lovely, please take this note to my father, you can go and see your family. That is an order, you haven't seen them in weeks. You deserve a break…'

'They won't let me. Besides, I'm your personal maid, therefore, I need to stay with you or close so if you need anything I am around to get it for you'

'There are heaps of different maids that can assist me. But keep in mind, you are more than just a maid to me, Roseanne. You're a friend. A friend that needs a break to see her beautiful family and friends''

'Thank you, my Queen,' she replied shyly.

'Remember, you can call me Julieanne. Please go and take a break?' I replied with a smile.

'Ok…' she replied, taking the note and heading out to find my father.

She is so lovely and thoughtful. I thought to myself.

In five minutes my father is going to storm through that door and command me to know why I turned down Roseanne's help and why I gave her time off. This is going to be fun…

'Julieanne???' called my father, coming down the hallway to my room.

'Hello, father. What do I owe the pleasure of your visit?' I asked with a sly smile.

'Why did you reject the help of your maid?' he asked furiously.

'Roseanne. And because I didn't need or want her help. I am more than capable of handling and packing my bag without assistance'

'And why on earth did you send her home for the weekend? She needs to be here, working'

'She NEEDS to be with her family and friends. Not working 24/7. Everyone deserves a break'

'Maids do not require such trivial things, they can sleep and eat here. I don't know what is so bad about that'

'It is terrible, they never see their family and friends. It's inhuman and I will not have it in my kingdom'

'Julieanne, must I remind you that there are standards that need to be upheld?' he asked, submissively.

'I am well aware of the standards of my kingdom. I am also now aware that I am the Queen and I should have the same amount of respect and power as my husband. I am capable of making my own rules, and ensuring that my people are looked after is my main priority. Everything else will come in time. But for the time being, it is not your place to command my workers and people to do anything, especially against my wishes or my husband's. You may be a dear friend to the former king, but you hold no power when it comes to my rules, my people, my life. So, I beg you, stop trying to ensure my life is miserable'

'I am not trying to make your life miserable, Julieanne. It is my job to make sure you understand what you are doing and that you are taking care of yourself. But it is also my job to foresee how the staff are working and that the people are kept in line'

'That is my responsibility as much as it is yours. I will sort over all of our rules and I will be making some changes, whether you approve or not. And I will not be taking these things to the voting table, if it is a rule that affects the people, then they shall vote for themselves. I am the Queen, father. I need to start acting like one'

***

Perfect. I thought to myself.

Julieanne reminds me a bit of myself, wanting to change people's views and the rules that we live under. Maybe that is why I am having so much fun writing the novel? Even if it will never get published.

I have always felt like the world is unjust and inhuman in many ways, from the way people are treated to the political rules and regulations that we need to follow. To the jobs that we are allowed and expected to get. Like the unjustness of the inequality of women and men. Whose life should be equal and fair, not making one sex more dishonored and less than the other?

'Emma? Can you come down to the kitchen please?' called Ma.

'Coming Ma!' I replied.

'What can I do?' I asked.

'Darling, can you please help me prepare for supper?'

'Sure'

As I helped her Ma prepare for supper, I couldn't help but wonder why Ma was suddenly acting like anything was fine, that the family was fine, that the whole world was now fine.

'Ma? You've been in a good mood lately'

'Yes, well you cannot be depressed all the time'

'Why are you in a good mood?'

'Because my family is finally healing, so it is the town'

'Yes, but the newspaper, you, and I are all still receiving hateful telegrams over the article I wrote about the mining accident'

'Yes, that is true. But we are stronger than the world thinks. And besides that, it will pass. If the world knows that we are affected by their harsh, cruel words then they will continue to send them, if they think we have moved on and aren't affected by it then they are more than likely going to stop'

'I don't think that is the way it works'

'It is'

'Have you moved on from Pa?'

'No, of course not! I think about him every minute of every day. But I have accepted the fact that he is gone, he won't be coming home. And he wouldn't want us being depressed for the rest of our lives'

'It has only been 3 months, that isn't a long time'

'No, but it is enough time to heal and accept the facts, Emma'

'Ma? Emma? What are you talking about? Do you not love Pa anymore??' asked Maybelle from the doorway.

'No, of course we still love him,' I replied.

'Yes, what Emma said is true, Maybelle. I think it is time that we all moved forward as a family'

'You may have given up on him and his life, but I haven't! I will not stop missing him, I will not stop mourning his death, I will not stop sitting by a photograph! I won't!'

'Maybelle, darling. We aren't telling you to move on or to forget him. But I think it is time to move past his death, celebrate his life with us, move past grief and mourning, and start to smile more, laughing even. Moving forward isn't forgetting. And as your sister has written, death may be terrible, but it is also beautiful. Isn't that right, Emma?'

'I guess so...'

'I will not move on! I can't!' Maybelle cried before storm-ing off to her room.

'Let me talk to her, Ma' I quickly say before Ma can chase her to the room, and scold her for slamming the door.

'Ok...' Ma replied at a loss.

Knock...Knock...

'Maybelle? May I come in?' I asked.

'Sure' she sobbed.

'Why...is Ma...b...eing so...difficult?' she asked between sobs.

'She is just telling you that it is ok to move forward, to forgive him for leaving, to stop grieving'

'But...I...d...don't...want to...s...stop'

'And you don't have to, Ma is just worried is all'

'Why?'

'Because she wants us to be happy, it upsets her when we are upset...'

'But she shoul...d...also be upset,' she continued.

'Yes, and she is. But she is very good at not showing it, she will always miss Pa. Maybelle, that will never change, we all will. But it is okay to live your life, to smile and laugh, to go out and explore. Pa wouldn't want you to continue to lock yourself up in the house all the time'

'Pa isn't here, so how do you know what he wants?'

'I just do, ok?'

'But how? You can't speak to the dead!'

'No, of course I can't. Do you trust me?'

'Yes'

'Then trust me when I say that moving on is not forgetting, he will always be with us. Ok?'

'Ok...I guess you're right...' she replied with a grim smile.

'I hope you understand the difference between it and that Ma isn't saying it to be nasty' I replied before embracing

Maybelle in a tight hug before exiting the room. 'I love you'
I continued before closing the door.

CHAPTER TEN

*D*earest Ben,

I miss you so much! When can you get time off to come and visit me and Brendan? He is making me go crazy!

The town hasn't been the same since you left, it seems lonelier, too.

I am sorry to hear about your friend, I wish I was there to support you more. It must be hard on everyone, especially her family, who, I am sure, loved her very much and will miss her dearly. If there is any way for me to help, please let me know!

The complaints are coming through daily, people disrespecting me or my writing. But that has become something I am used to! While I still receive some shocking telegrams, most are repetitive. So that makes it easier to deal with, or some don't have the correct grammar or even sentence structure. Or the handwriting is so bad that I can't even read it. But the general theme throughout all is that females should not be permitted to write, at any level. And that it should be left to the professionals (males). This viewpoint is horrid. I don't understand why it is such a sin to have a female novelist, but apparently it is. And I currently cannot speak up about our segregated society, especially with everything that has happened. It just doesn't feel like the right time, but to be honest, I don't think it will ever be the right time.

Anyway, I hope things improve there, I look forward to our next visit! I haven't seen you in almost 6 months! That's far too long to be apart!

Looking forward to your reply, Benny.

Love,

Emma

***

'Emma?'

'Maybelle, you can come in,' I replied from my desk.

'Sorry, I wasn't sure if you were in the middle of writing something'

'Nope, I just finished writing a telegram to Ben. I am just about to start writing an article'

'Oh, cool...did you want me to go then?' she asked.

'No, it's fine'

'Are you sure? I don't want to bother you'

'You are never a bother, Maybelle. What's wrong?'

'I just needed someone to talk to'

'About what?'

'I've been having bad dreams lately about Pa. They won't stop...'

'Oh, have you spoken to Ma about this?'

'No, she will just tell me to move on...I mean it happened months ago. Almost 6 months ago...'

'No, she won't. She just wants to make sure you are ok is all'

'Yeah, I know. But sometimes I think she worried too much'

'She wants what's best for you, don't be too hard on her'

'Yeah, I know...'

'Talk to her, Maybelle. See what she says and you never know, she might surprise you with her answer'

'Maybe...'

'Definitely, but for now, I need to write this article'

'What's it about?'

'The change in leadership in Hillstone'

'The town a little ways past the river?'

'Yes, that's the one'

'But what happened to their other leader?'

'He stepped down due to retirement and his health decreasing'

'Who's taking his place?'

'His brother. Since he doesn't have a son, the brother is the next town leader. Once he retires it will go to the brother's son'

'When will the people get a vote?'

'The men will vote when there is no other heir to the leadership, or if the heir refuses to become the town leader then the men will get the chance to vote'

'Why can't we vote?'

'Women don't get to vote, since the men decided that they will have a more influential say in what happens. Thankfully, our town isn't so uptight about society's views on women, but most of society is not as respectful as our town leader'

'So, the world doesn't respect or like women?'

'Women are segregated and are expected to be housewives'

'Segregated? So, what if we want to not stay home and be housewives?'

'Then there are selected jobs that we can choose from, and even then there aren't many options. We can become teachers, nannies, seamstresses, and midwives. But we must marry and bear children to continue to have these privileges. Otherwise, we will lose any more respect that the town will have for us'

'That doesn't sound fair...'

'It isn't. But it is the life that we live, whether we like it or not'

'Can't we decide to change that?'

'Yes, but that would cause chaos, and we would lose privileges and respect. You need to secure a safe place with society to be able to challenge the rights that we have. To challenge the societal views that dictate and control our lives'

'That's terrible, well enjoy writing your article, Emma'

'Thanks, now go and speak to Ma'

'Fine'

'Thank you'

***

Retirement of Mayor of Hillstone

It has come to my attention that the current Mayor of Hillstone has just announced his retirement, forwarding the responsibility to his brother, Micah.

While this may come as a shock to some, the current Mayor has been stepping back and allowing his brother to take part in the town's ruling, this was the first indication of his planned retirement.

The current Mayor looked after Hillstone for more than 60 years, making him one of the longest Mayor's in

Hillstone's history. This in turn means that Micah has big shoes to fit into. While Micah is the youngest of the brothers, he is also the most fitting to look after Hillstone, with his siblings' health deteriorating over time and since his sister is unfit for the job, the only other person able to inherit the job is Micah before passing it on to his child. Currently, Micah only has a daughter, therefore, she will be deemed unfit for the job. Micah and his family will need to hope for a son in order to continue their family's line as town Mayor. The Charleston Family has been the longest family to ever hold the Mayor title, therefore, it would be terrible for the family to end that legacy, and for their future generations will need to be voted in by the town rather than inheriting the title and the responsibility.

While the retirement of the current Mayor is tragic, the town is hopeful that Micah will continue his older brother's promises and continue to make the town of Hillstone a better place for all.

Written by:

Emma Hicks

Once I finished writing my article, I found myself staring out the window and admiring the wildlife that was just trying to survive the summer. Always looking for food and water. Finding water would be the hardest, simply because it doesn't rain here often, so most waterholes dry up over the summer from the scorching heat.

***

'Is Emma around?' asked Kyle.

'Hello, Kyle. I haven't seen you in a while' Ma questioned, not even trying to mask her dislike for him.

'Yeah, I've been busy'

'Doing?'

'Working on the farm'

'So, let me get this right, you are incapable of stopping by while working on the farm? So, why are you here?'

'I'm here to see Emma, Mrs Hicks'

'Emma is busy'

'Can you please go and get her?'

'Why'

'Mrs Hicks, I do not have all day. I need to discuss something with Emma'

'What is so important that you need to speak with her about? You ignored her for the past year. And now, out of the blue, you would like to talk with her?'

'Yes, please'

'Kyle? What are you doing here' I interrupted from behind her Ma in the doorframe.

'Emma, do you have a minute?'

'Depends, why?'

'I just need to talk'

'Clearly, Emma doesn't want to talk to you, goodbye' replied Mrs Hicks irruptly.

'Ma...it's fine. Why don't you go and make some tea? I believe Maybelle might need to talk to you also'

'But—'

'Ma, please'

'Ok, I'll go. Coffee or tea?'

'Tea please, Ma'

'She always likes that?' he asked once I had closed the door, and Ma was far out of reach to hear what we were saying.

'Let's go for a short walk, then you can tell me the exact reason you are here' I instructed before continuing as I began walking 'And you know very well why Ma doesn't like you and why she doesn't want me to talk to you, so why ask such a stupid question?'

'I thought she may have had a change of heart, after all, it has been a year'

'Yes, but after everything that has happened, it cannot be easily forgotten or forgiven'

'If you say so...'

'I do'

'I figured as much'

'So, what do you want?'

This would have been a nice walk if it wasn't for the poor company... I thought to myself as she waited for Kyle's reply.

'Right, well, I needed to talk to you about something that I am going to need a serious answer for. And you are not to laugh. It isn't a laughing matter, understood?' he responds.

'One, I do not take orders from you. Two, get to the point' I replied coolly.

'I need you to marry me' he blurted out.

'You what!?!' I laughed, in absolute shock at this outrageous request. *I don't even know how to reply to that.* I thought.

'I told you not to laugh!'

'And I told you, I do not take orders from you. Why on earth would I marry you?'

'Because we are compatible, my Ma likes you. And with Pa being the way he is, I need to marry in order to take over the family business and get my inheritance'

'So...you want me to marry you so you get your family name and inheritance? You do understand that I am not some item or damsel in distress that needs to marry to be satisfied in life? And besides, I already have someone'

'Brendan? You're going to marry him? His Ma's crazy and he's not much better!' he exclaimed.

'He's Ma is not crazy! And Brendan is a really great guy, unlike you'

'Ouch...I think that is meant to hurt my feelings?'

'Take it as you wish, but do you honestly think I'd ever agree to marry you? And that Ma would allow it?'

'Generally speaking, it is our Pa's that decide who marries who. But since yours is dead, I guess that means another male will need to dictate who you marry'

'Unfortunately, for you at least, I don't have any other males that have that right, therefore, it will then be the choice of my Ma. So, I stand by my original statement. Ma would never allow it'

'We shall see about that, Emma'

'Emma?!?' called Brendan from behind us.

'Hey, B'

'What are you doing with *him*?' asked Brendan through his teeth.

'He requested that I speak to him about some urgent issue. But it isn't urgent either way'

'What about?' he questioned.

'Oh, I'm glad you asked, *Brendan*. I am just asking for her hand in marriage' explained Kyle.

'Oh...is that so?' Brendan questioned.

'So? B, what do you think I said?'

'Well, thank you for your time Emma, my Pa will be drafting up our marriage agreements and I will drop by in the next couple of weeks for you and your Ma to sign' dismissing himself before I had a chance to argue my case.

I hate the way Brendan is currently looking at me like I've disappointed him. The look of pure hurt and disapproval. A look I don't like seeing on anyone's face, especially those I love.

'So, you will marry him?'

'What? Of course, I won't! That's absurd!'

'He surely seemed to think you agree with the idea!'

'He's delusional!'

'Coming from the girl that dated him! For two years!'

'That was over a year ago! And I've told you how that ended!'

'Oh, right, with him completely ignoring you!?'

'Yes! I don't know what else you expect me to say!' I yelled. I can feel the tears welling up in my eyes, waiting patiently to be let fall.

'I've got to go...Ma is expecting me' he replied a little softer.

'B...?' I whispered as he turned around and left.

CHAPTER ELEVEN

It has been almost a week since my encounter with Kyle, and a week since Brendan last spoke to me. I think this is the longest time that we have gone without speaking.

'Emma?!'

'Coming, Ma!' I called.

As I headed for the dining room I wondered what Brendan and I would be doing if Kyle hadn't shown up. Would we be happy? Would we be down at the fields cuddling until the sunset and nightfall enveloped us?

'Have you spoken to Brendan yet?' she asked as I appeared in the doorway.

'No...'

'Why not?'

'How many times do you want to have this conversation?'

'As long as it takes for you to talk to him'

'That could be months from now, Ma. We have had this conversation almost every day since'

'Yes, and we will continue to have this conversation. Kyle shouldn't be able to come between you and Brendan, I won't allow it'

'Ma, this isn't something you can magically fix'

'I can and will try'

'But why? What is the point?'

'The point is that you and Brendan are perfect for each other, and you are miserable without him'

'Sure, do you want me to agree? Do you want me to pretend that I am fine?'

'No, of course not'

'Then why are you insisting that I move forward? That I be the one to talk to him first? I have done nothing wrong, so what should I be apologising for?'

'Were you not the one going for a walk with Kyle? And failing to argue when he mentioned filling out the marriage paperwork, with Brendan standing next to you?'

'He had already left! How could I argue a point if he wasn't listening and wasn't there to let me!?'

'You could have gone after him'

'Then I would have left Brendan!'

'Stop yelling at me, Emma!' she scolded.

'I will do as I wish with my time and my life, I am sorry that I am a disappointment to you!' I yelled back.

'You are not a disappointment! But you need to discuss this all with Brendan so he understands what is happening! That way you are going, you won't have anyone to marry before the end of the year! Is that what you want?'

'No, of course not! I need to get back to writing' I replied coolly.

Why does she need to get involved? I've got it all under control! Right, I need to calm down, I have a novel to write. I thought to myself.

***

'Queen Julieanne, are you in here?' asked Roseanne.

'Yes, Roseanne, please come in,' I replied warmly.

'Your father asked me to give this to
you...' she replied as she handed me a
piece of paper that read.

Julieanne, you are required to attend this afternoon's meeting. This
is not up for debate. Please dress
appropriately. And be on your best
behaviour. I will be attending, and so
will the former king and your husband,
as well as some other official members
of the court. This meeting is very
important, and it is of utmost im-
portance that you attend. This ruling
will impact you as well as the people
of this Kingdom. You cannot pick and
choose which meetings you will be
attending, that is not your place, and
it is your responsibility as Queen.

sincerely, your father.

'Great, such as a warm letter…' I spoke coolly.

'I didn't read it, my Queen. But given your relationship with your father, I bet it would be all about business?'

'Yes, it always is with him. Always talking to me about my responsibilities and my obligations. As if I didn't already know them'

'He's only trying to help'

'Yes, I am well aware. But I do think he holds too much power over the rulings in this Kingdom, but I appreciate his assistance'

'Well, my Queen, you can always assign the court's representatives'

'That would require more meetings than I have time for, and how many times do I need to remind you, you don't need to call me 'Queen'. Julieanne works quite fine for me'

'Yes, I understand that. But you are my Queen so I will address you as such'

'Is there anything I can say to make you reconsider?'

'No'

'Okay, Roseanne, I respect your wishes. But I need to start getting ready for the meeting, otherwise, my father will be angry if I turn up late. Especially since it is not really ladylike or queenlike for that matter'

'Very true, my Queen. Please call me if you need anything'

'I will, thank you' I replied as Roseanne left the room, leaving me to ponder my life choices and my plan for this afternoon's meeting.

***

Right, I have an article to begin writing, about next month being the last month of autumn for the year.

The End of Another Autumn

As most of you are aware, the seasons are once again changing and are becoming colder as we approach winter.

I am writing this article to remind everyone to clean out their fireplaces, whilst we do not get snow here, it does get cold as the sun sets.

The main thing that you need to remember is to keep warm.

Enjoy the remaining months of autumn with family and friends. And prepare for another beautiful winter wonderland!

Written by,

Emma Hicks

'Emma! When are you planning on coming out of your room?!' called Ma.

'When I am finished with my writing tasks for the day!' I called back.

'It's almost supper! You should have finished them already!'

'I would be if you stopped interrupting me!' I called back, irritated.

'You better come out for supper!' Ma yelled.

'Fine!' I yelled back.

I hate being mad at her, but she doesn't have the right to dictate how I act when it comes to my relationships. I thought as I reached for a notepad to start writing my telegram to Ben.

Dearest Ben,

I hope everything is going well for you, I am still waiting for you to come and visit. I miss having you around, especially lately. I could have really used your support.

I am currently fighting with Brendan and Ma about my marriage. Kyle came out of nowhere and demanded that I marry him, and since Pa is no longer here to say 'no' Ma and I have to come up with another way to deceive our petty systematics.

Brendan seems convinced that I will marry Kyle and not him, and I haven't spoken to him in about a week. Which is killing me. I do understand a little as to where he is coming from, but he should also know by now that I have no intentions of marrying Kyle. And I never have wanted to.

Anyway, besides all of that, I have written about half of my novel which has been fun. The widespread media still won't leave me be about my writing about the mining incident, but my town seems to have moved forward, thankfully. I hope they will stop soon though, it is getting annoying.

I hope everything is working out for you, you deserve so much!

I wish I was there with you, we could have had so much fun and I wish I could write alongside you again, that was always an amazing time.

Maybelle has been getting more and more jobs which she seems to be enjoying, it is keeping her mind off Pa. Ma has begun work again, and she wanted to make sure everything was ok at home before returning. My teas have become more in demand, which is amazing but also very stressful as I now have people from other towns putting orders in, which means I have to work extra hard to make sure all of the teas are ready on time. My soap business is also going amazing. I think I am now supplying soap to every household in town, and have also begun extending to other towns, which will be a challenge. But I am always looking for new ways to create the things I love and to see people when they collect them is amazing.

So, life is all bad here. But it has obviously been better. The town is still mourning the losses from the mines, and we have begun finding a new mining spot so we can continue to support our town as well as the other local towns, so it should be interesting. They won't be able to find one for a couple more months yet, but hopefully it doesn't take too long.

Love always,

Emma x

***

'Emma, can you please pass me the salt?' asked Maybelle as we sat around the dining table.

'Of course,' I replied with a small smile on my face.

'So, Maybelle...how was school?' Ma questioned, carefully.

'It was ok, I guess. We didn't really learn any new stuff. Just old stuff. So, that wasn't every entertaining'

'That's annoying, they should be teaching you about stuff that actually matters, not reteaching you stuff you already know and understand'

'I guess...' Maybelle replied while she moved her food from one spot to another in her place.

'Stop playing with your food and eat it, Maybelle. You know better than to waste food' Ma scolded.

'So, Emma, did you write much today?' asked Ma.

'Same as usual,' I replied.

'You could give me more information. I have done nothing wrong here'

'Of course, you haven't. You wouldn't be able to tell even if you did'

'Emma! I have had enough of this attitude!'

'Well, you're the one that commanded I attend supper'

'Attending supper and being disrespectful are two completely different things, and you know that Emma'

'I am well aware of the difference. However, I am also aware that I am not being disrespectful and you are the one raising your voice at me' I quipped back.

'Can you both please stop arguing?' interrupted Maybelle.

'Sorry, honey. Are you enjoying your meal?' asked Ma, with a smile plastered onto her face.

'Yes, thank you'

'May I be excused?' I asked.

'Where are you going?' Ma questioned.

'For a walk'

'A night? In winter? Are you insane?'

'My insanity must come from you' I spoke coolly as I rose from the table and headed for the front door, while Ma continued to protest at the idea.

I should probably care more about what she is telling me to do, but today I am not in the mood. I need to go for a walk and relax my mind. Otherwise, I am pretty sure I'd lose my mind being locked in that house any longer. Things have definitely changed within our house since Pa passed, Ma seems colder and strict. And Maybelle is gloomy and depressed. I hate it. But apparently, it cannot be changed. Hopefully, this walk will end these restless thoughts and allow me to finally have a good night's sleep rather than continually worrying...hopefully.

CHAPTER TWELVE

*D*earest Em,

Please stop avoiding me. I have told you that I am sorry about the way I acted. It has been nearly 3 weeks since I last spoke to you. I understand that you are angry with me and probably Kyle. Please remember, that only you can decide who you marry, the rules and regulations have never worried you before when it comes to issues of your own happiness or your families.

I am not too sure why you are still avoiding me completely, but I am sure you have your own reasons and I respect that. But please give me something, I don't care if it is just a letter saying to leave you alone for a while longer...I would hate it, but I would do it. I know that you have a lot going on, please let me help you get through it all. We have been through so much together already, and I will always be around if and when you require help.

I love you forever and always. Never forget that.

I am sure Kyle is still begging for your hand in marriage, and I know you don't want that. So, we need to work out a way around it. I heard a rumor that Kyle has just finished processing the documents with his signature and his parents, so now they just need you and Mrs. Hicks to sign before anything can go further. But you and I both know that the town's officials can force you to sign the agreement whether you want to or not. Please let me in so we can work all of this out.

You, Em, make me the happiest man alive! I don't know what I would do without you, I think I'm already going crazy without talking to you. I know I have told you this a hundred times before, but I will say it again. Without you in my life there is no point in me living, I couldn't survive without you. And I don't want to imagine living without you and watching you marry another man, especially Kyle.

Apologies for my messy handwriting, I will work on it for you...

Yours always,

B xx

This is the seventh time I have read over Brendan's letter in an hour...pondering whether or not I will write out a reply, and what I would respond with.

'Emma?' Maybelle's voice echoed through the door into my cold, empty room.

'Come in, Maybelle' I replied, warmly before continuing 'What do you want?'

'I just wanted to see how you are doing. Ma said you received a letter from Brendan, have you replied?'

'Yes I did, but no I haven't replied'

'Why not?'

'Because I don't know whether I want to yet and I don't know what to say'

'Well, I am sure you will come up with something amazing, but you should really reply to him'

'I might, once I figure out what to say...why does it bother you so much?'

'Because you seem so unhappy, I don't like that. And Brendan seems to make you happy so please, reply to him'

'Fine...' I gave in before she left my room, leaving me to dwell on my dilemma about what I was planning on writing to Brendan.

Dearest B,

I am sorry for not replying to you, but I needed time to refresh my memory and work out what I am planning on doing about my marriage arrangements.

If you wish to help me with avoiding the wedding arrangements for Kyle, then it might be best for you to stop by the house so we can address all of the issues at one time.

I have repeatedly told Kyle that I will not marry him, but like usual, he isn't listening and is doing his own thing either way.

Thank you for your letter, and all of the others before this one. Maybelle insisted that I reply to your letter. So, that is what I am doing.

I hope that you are aware of how petty you were behaving, but I also hope that you are aware of where I am coming from. If we cannot find a way around the arrangements then I will be forced to marry Kyle, something that I really don't want to happen. I expect this letter to arrive to you before the end of the day, especially since Jerry puts my letters and telegrams as top priority over the others in town. Therefore, as soon as I send this to you, it won't be long before you get it.

While we still have quite a bit that we need to discuss and work through, however, hopefully, we can put our issues aside so I can figure out how to prevent this disastrous wedding from occurring.

Love,

Em xx

Right, with that done, it should only be around an hour or so before Jerry arrives and he sends it to Brendan. Once he gets it, he will probably rush over here. Great...just what I wanted to do with my day. I thought as I sealed Brendan's letter and wrote his name.

With the letter finally out of the way, I need to figure out what I am going to do about the issue of Ma being angry with me...something tells me I cannot just write her an apology letter and be done with it. Especially since I live with her. But I need to find some way to make up for my behaviour and stubbornness towards her, something that should come easily. But it doesn't.

***

Brendan arrived at the front door of the house at midday, thankfully I was the only one home. Well, at least I believe that is a positive thing.

Brendan has been sitting in the living room for about half an hour, we are yet to actually talk. So, I left to make some coffee for us both, I thought it might help. Brendan and I have never been so awkward around each other before we always knew what to say, and what needed to be said. But today, neither of us knew the words that we wanted to express to one another. So, I decided to start with the basics, hopefully, that will result in some sort of normality.

'So...how's things?' I asked as I reentered the room and handed him his coffee.

'Not so great, but I am hoping I can amend things with you. That will be one less thing I will need to worry about' he replied, sipping his coffee. 'That is if you would like to amend things?'

'Of course, I do—' I started before realising that I actually have no idea how to respond to that question. 'But, I would like to ensure that we work out a way to stop this disastrous wedding from happening also?' I continued.

'That sounds like an amazing plan,' he smiled.

'Right, let me grab the documents addressing what Kyle wants me to sign off too, I'll also grab some paper and a quill so we can write ideas down' I replied before leaving to fetch the items.

Once I returned with my list I found Brendan standing by the window with a worried expression on his face.

'What's wrong?' I asked carefully, not wanting to upset him further.

'Kyle is waiting by your front door...what happens if we cannot stop this wedding?' he replied cautiously.

'Well, I would be forced to marry Kyle, and I couldn't be with you. Now, if you would excuse me, I'll just get rid of him. Be right back, don't go anyway...ok?'

Brendan smiled as I exited the room to go and find out whatever hell Kyle would like to enlighten me with today.

'Kyle' I gestured once I left the house, closing the door behind me. 'What are you doing here?' I continued.

'Can I not come and see my bride?' he inquired.

'I am not your bride...at least not yet. So, please just answer my question. What are you doing here?' I repeated.

'I am here to ask, once again, for you to sign these papers so the wedding can be underway'

'I told you yesterday, I will not be signing anything until my Ma and I have sorted a couple things out for ourselves. I don't believe I need your approval to do that. I have a week to sign the papers or find a way out. So, I will use whatever time I have left to do exactly that. Please be on your way, I have things I need to do'

'Is it true? That you and Brendan have ended things?'

'I've got no idea who told you that, but my guess is that the townsfolk are talking. As for my relationship with Brendan is concerned, it has nothing to do with anyone except Brendan, and I'

'Well Darling, I will be seeing you at the altar'

'Not if I can help it'

Why does he need to make this so much more difficult? Why can't he just leave me until I have sorted it all out? Anyway, I need to sort through everything with Brendan and work out how to escape this wedding... I thought.

'How did that happen?' questions Brendan as soon as I arrived in the living room.

'He's gone,' I replied matter-of-factly.

'What did he want?'

'He was asking for me to sign the marriage agreement, the same thing he wanted yesterday...' I stated. 'So, what's the plan on how to stop the wedding so he can finally leave me alone?' I asked.

'That is a very good question...however, I am not too sure on the answer to that...'

'Well, we better get to work then...'

As Brendan and I tossed ideas back and forth I couldn't help but wonder what it would be like if Pa was still here. Would he cancel the wedding arrangements? Would he think that Kyle was the best suited to be my husband? Did he have a plan in place that he could enact? Unfortunately, all of these questions are pointless. And they wouldn't amount to anything, since they wouldn't be answered.

'What about convincing Kyle that there is someone else he can marry in town?' he suggested.

'I've tried convincing him of that. But, unfortunately, he has his mind set on marrying me and so does his Pa. So, that isn't even an option' I replied 'But maybe, we can convince his Pa that this is all a bad idea?'

'If Kyle is the one that left you to begin with, I bet it wasn't his original idea to marry you. It would have come from his Pa. Therefore, arguing with him wouldn't work'

'Point taken' I sighed.

Right before I had planned on giving up for the day Maybelle and Ma appeared in the doorway, eyeing us suspiciously.

'Welcome home' I announced.

'What are you guys working on?' Ma asked as Maybelle waved, then began to head to her room.

'We are trying to figure out a way that I can get out of this wedding, would your help be appreciated?' I asked 'I mean, really, really appreciated. I'm just about out of ideas. And I really don't want to have to marry him, especially if I can help it' I continued without breaking eye contact.

'I suppose I can help before starting on supper' she replied.

She is still annoyed by the way I have treated her over the last couple of weeks, so I am surprised she agreed at all.

'Well, this is everything that Brendan and I have thought of today,' I say as I hand her the list 'I don't think any of them will work out though, but maybe you can find one that you think might work?' I continued to be hopeful.

'Yes...I shall look at this list. I am glad you too are bad on talking terms. Maybe Emma can stop acting like an arrogant child' she scolded.

'Sorry about that'

'Your sorry now because you want my help'

'I am sorry, I have been sorry the whole time but I didn't know how to apologize correctly'

'So, asking for my help is your way of apologizing?'

'No, of course not. I will find a way to make it up to you. But right now, I have a wedding to stop'

'Of course, it is more important isn't it?'

'You know what I mean...' I whined 'Is there anything on the list that would work?'

'Probably not. Keep thinking up ideas, I have to help Maybelle with some things' ' she replied coolly as she rose and walked out of the room.

Well, that went well... I thought.

'So, what did you do to Mrs. Hicks to get her this mad at you?' asked Brendan.

'Everything. Right, I think it is time for us to leave this wedding stuff for today. I have a couple of articles and telegrams to write and post tomorrow, then I'll look into more ideas' I replied 'So, it is best if you came back around 2 tomorrow' I continued.

'Sounds like a plan. So, should we discuss everything that happened between us...?'

'Probably, did you want to go for a walk then?'

'Isn't Mrs. Hicks about to start cooking supper?'

'Yes, but we have some time before supper time'

'Ok, let's sort through our issues, shall we?'

'right...' I replied as I rose 'I hope we can work everything out' I continued as we headed for the front door, ready to spill our guts to each other.

CHAPTER THIRTEEN

After a night of tossing and turning, I finally saw the sun rising outside my window. It is such a splendid sight, I love it. While I don't generally see it rise completely, as in winter it rises at around 5:30 am. I wish I was able to sleep, but as soon as the sun is awake, so am I. I can never sleep during the day, and since there is too much light, I won't be able to sleep now. I think this was one of my worst sleep since Pa died 8 months ago.

Well, since I am awake I may as well write out my daily to-do list. How exciting. I thought as I rose and headed for my desk and began writing out my list.

To-Do List:

- Tidy room

- Write more on novel

- Write out another article

- Work out the marriage situation! IMPORTANT!

- Apologise to Ma

- Make some teas and soaps

Once I completed my to-do list, I headed to the fireplace and lit it up. I love the feeling of the fire's warmth brushing against the cold chill of winter's air. It's a welcoming warmth. One I will always treasure.

Maybe I should grab a book to read while I wait for Ma's return? I mean there isn't really anything else I can do about the wedding at the moment. I thought to myself as I headed for my bookshelf and pulled off *Persuasion by Jane Austen.* One of my all-time favorites, I don't even know how many times I have read it.

As I made my way back to the fireplace I couldn't help but wonder what I was going to do if I married Brendan, there was still so much that I didn't know or that I was unsure of. But, that is a problem for later, no point stressing over something I cannot change yet.

Right, no point thinking about any of that now, it is time to read.

***

'Emma! Have you seen my school book!' called Maybelle from the kitchen.

'No,' I called back as I headed out to help her look 'Where did you last have it?' I asked.

'I don't remember, Ma and I were looking over some notes a couple of days ago with it'

'Maybe ask her where it is?'

'She's still sleeping'

'So, she is sleeping and you decided it was a good idea to yell for me?' I asked quizzically.

'I didn't think it through. I need this book'

'We will find it, Ma is probably awake now. Why don't you go and ask if she has seen it?'

'ok...' she replied, shyly 'But what if she doesn't know where it is either?'

'It will be around here somewhere'

As I stand in the living room, I can actually see all of the things that have changed since Pa's passing. There are things that are missing and things that are moved. This is something big in this house, we don't move anything and we, generally, don't lose anything. Ma is far too organized for that to happen, I guess I get that trait from her. But, Pa was always the one person in the house who often got scolded for moving something, it seems that Maybelle has gotten that from him.

'Have you found it?' I called Maybelle.

'Yes, Ma had it in her room!' she called back.

I knew Ma would know where it was, granted I didn't expect it to be with her...I guess Ma has a lesson for Maybelle about leaving her stuff lying around the house.

A knock pounded at the door, startling me from my thoughts.

Right before I reached the door they knocked again. 'Anyone home?!' they called.

'Coming!' I answered when I reached the door and pulled it open to find Jerry standing before me.

"ello Emma, how are you?' he asked casually.

'Hello, Jerry. I'm well thank you, are those for me?' I asked, pointing to the letter he was holding.

'Sure are, I believe there is one from Ben...' he smiled warmly.

'Oh, thank you!' I replied as I hastily grabbed the letter from him 'Goodbye, I'll see you tomorrow, thanks again!'

'Goodbye, enjoy' he replied as I shut the door and headed towards my room where I plopped on the bed, tearing open Ben's telegram.

The telegram read;

Dearest Emma,

Unfortunately, I won't be able to make it next week, so I have been called into a meeting. I will be free the following week, hopefully, it will stay free. Will keep you updated.

I hope that you are all well.

Kyle is being absurd if he thinks you will marry him, I am sure you will find a way out of it. You always do.

I have missed having you around, but you will get there. I have met some amazing people, and my job is going well. I am always being called into meetings though, which isn't as fun as being able to write.

I hope you and Mrs. Hicks can work out your differences and become happy again. That is the same with Brendan, he would be foolish to let you go without fighting it.

I have done some research here for how to get out of a forced marriage, and have included the article in this telegram. I hope it helps, sorry I am not there to support you, but please send me something if there is anything I can do to help!

Love always,
Ben x

Ben's telegrams are always the sweetest. I thought to myself as I looked over the article.

Dearest Benny,

I think you have figured it out! It says in the article that a couple of years back a young lady was forced into marriage, but managed to get out of it because she married someone else! That's all I need to do! So, I need to mend things with Brendan and marry him, since he is the only one that I would want to marry. You're a genius! How did I not think of that? I don't know what I would do without you! You literally saved my life big time!

I am glad everything is going well for you! And yeah, meetings sound terrible, but I am sure you are the best that they have, which is why they keep asking for you to join them.

I do want to see you, but please don't feel sorry about not being able to make it. I appreciated the notice though. Work is more important, you can visit anytime!

I could keep writing for hours, however, I need to call Brendan and see what he thinks of this amazing plan of yours! If this works, I'd be forever in your debt!

Thank you!

Love Always,

Emma

'Ma! Can I use the telephone?' I called.

'Sure!' she called back 'Who are you calling?' she questioned.

'Brendan! I think I have a way to stop my forced marriage! I'll tell you once you return from the markets!' I called back.

'Ok...I love you! Talk soon' she called back before stepping out into the would be blissful sunny weather, except the wind was colder than usual.

Right, now how am I going to explain all of this to Brendan?
I Emma as I dialed his number.

'Hello?' he answered.

'Hey, B. Do you want to come over? I think I worked out a way to save my wedding plans'

'I can be over in half an hour if that works?'

'Yes, that's fine. Everything ok?'

'I'll explain later'

'Ok, goodbye B'

'Goodbye Em'

Oh, how I hate the limited telephone time we have. It should have been longer so I could have just explained everything on the telephone, I thought.

***

'No, that's the thing, to do this we don't need our Pa's permission, as long as we have our Ma's permission I don't think it matters' I explained. Brendan arrived about half an hour ago and I explained the plan but he, of course, is skeptical.

'Are you sure this will work?'

'No, but isn't it worth a shot? If I'm married to you then I can't marry Kyle'

'Yes, which is logical. except, we would need to get the Pastor to agree to do the wedding'

'Yes, that would probably be the only hard part of all of this'

As Brendan nervously began pacing the room, I began to wonder what else had worried about.

'What's wrong? I asked, my curiosity getting the better of me.

'This wedding issue is what's wrong,' he replied, irritated.

'No. There is something else that you aren't telling me'

'It's nothing you need to worry about at the moment'

'Why won't you tell me?'

'Because you already have enough to worry about, it will only add to you worrying more'

'Fine, you do what you want either way right?'

'Why are you fighting me on this?' he snapped.

'Because you're not telling me anything!'

'Look, let's just focus on this wedding, we can work out our own problems later...ok?'

'Fine'

'Have you contacted Ben lately? Brendan asked, hoping to lighten the tense mood.

'Yes, I sent him a telegram this morning. " I replied coolly.

'How is he?' he pushed.

'He seems to be going well, he won't be able to come down next week though. He tried but got called into a meeting. But besides that, he seems to be going well'

'That's good, I'm glad'

'Yeah, so am I. Do you send him telegrams often?'

'Yeah, sometimes. Depending if I have the money or not'

'Fair enough, that makes sense'

'Yeah...so, if we are to get married we would probably need to talk about some boundaries?'

'Why can't we do that after we are married?'

'Because I would much rather go into the marriage without secrets'

'Ok...Oh, wait, are we expected to buy a house?'

'I believe so'

'Right, well I guess that is more of a later problem, considering we will need to see if we can get it all approved. And that both our parents agree to it. We can head over to yours now if you want to discuss it with your Ma?'

'Ah, no it's ok! I'll talk with her when I return home. When is your Ma coming home?'

'She will be home shortly, why don't you want me to see your Ma?'

'I do, she is just...busy at the moment'

'Right...' I replied skeptically 'But you are avoiding talking to her with me, so there is definitely something going on. But I am sure you will tell me eventually' I continued.

'Yes, I will. But not right now' he smiled before continuing, 'I don't and will never keep secrets from you, Em. You should know that by now'

'Yeah, I do. But you are also entitled to keep things to yourself. Therefore, you don't need to tell me everything'

'True but I want to' he replied before leaning forward and placing a soft, delicate kiss on my forehead.

'Than—'

'I'm home!' Ma called from the front door, cutting off what I was saying.

'Hello, let me help' I asked as I reached the door and grabbed some bags from her arms, Brendan followed my lead and did the same.

'Oh, Brendan, I'm glad you are here. And I am glad you and Emma finally sorted out your issues. She was too moody for my liking' Ma replied as she headed for the kitchen to help us unpack the groceries.

'I think I worked out a way for me to escape marrying Kyle...' I spoke carefully.

'Well...?' she questioned.

'All I would need to do is marry someone else before I need to marry Kyle' I started 'I cannot marry Kyle if I am married to someone else'

'Yes, that is very true. Brendan and you are a perfect couple, so I would be fine with it. But how do you plan on convincing the wedding officials to permit the wedding?'

How hard could it be? Pa saved his son's life, they owe our family one big favor'

'That is very true, but I don't know if they would be happy if you used that against them. And not to mention, Kyle and his Pa will be furious'

'Well, they would have had to know that I would find a way out of it. I always do'

'Ok. Get Brendan's Ma to agree and we will go from there, I will book an appointment with the wedding official and see what I can do'

CHAPTER FOURTEEN

'Emma, Kyle is at the door!' called Maybelle from the front of the house, she must have caught Kyle on her way out to school.

'Thank you!' I called back and headed to greet him.

'Kyle, what did you want?' I inquire.

'Your hand in marriage, we have five days until our wedding so therefore, I need you to sign the paperwork'

'Thank you for the unpleasant reminder, I will sign it when I am ready' I replied coolly, 'But until that point, I would appreciate it if you left me and my family alone'

'I will, for now. But as soon as it gets closer, I will be stopping by again'

'Fine' I replied as I shut the door, not even waiting for his reply. I don't want or need to hear what he has to say.

Right now, all I need to do is wait for Ma to finish her meeting with the wedding official, although she hasn't left yet. I also need to write a little article. Then that will be out of the way. All I need to worry about is the wedding. I thought out my daily tasks. I like to think of what I want to get done or I write them out so I don't forget them.

'Emma, I'm just heading out to visit the wedding officials and work out if I can convince them to wed you and Brendan. Did you need anything else requested?' Ma asked while packing up her bag, and getting ready to go.

'Not that I can think of, thank you for going down. I would have no idea what to say or how to act. When will you return home?'

'In about 2 hours, I believe. I'll let you know' she replied as she kissed me on the cheek and headed for the door, going on her merry way to convince the wedding officials to wed me to someone other than Kyle, this should be fun.

'Thank you, I will check in with Brendan about what his Ma thinks sometime today and to go over some of the fine prints' I replied.

***

Ring...ring...ring...

Argh, I hate how long the telephone takes to go through! And the talking time period! I thought while I waited for the telephone to go through.

'Hello?' asked Brendan, finally.

'Hey, it's Emma' I replied, relieved that it didn't take any longer.

'Oh, hey, Em. What's going on?' he questioned.

'Just wondering if you have spoken to your Ma yet?'

'Yes, I spoke with her briefly last night. She is fine with it all but she is unsure if she will be able to attend the wedding'

'Why not?'

'She hasn't been feeling well, I'll explain it all later'

'Ok, I love you'

'I love you too, Em. Good luck with the meeting today'

'Thank you, Ma is already there. I believe she is set to arrive home shortly'

'Nice, well goodbye, talk later'

'Ok, goodbye' I replied before hanging up.

***

'So, for me to be able to marry Brendan all I need to do is sign some papers and get you and Brendan, and his Ma to sign and agree?' I inquired to Ma 'That sounds a little too easy' I continued, Ma had been home for about an hour explaining how her meeting went.

'Yes, it does. This is why we will do everything step by step to ensure everything is done correctly and that we don't miss anything'

'When can we sign the paperwork?'

'Tomorrow'

'Wonderful, so what can I do for the remainder of my day?'

'Relax, there is nothing we can do until morning, so write on your novel or something'

'Hmmm...ok' I resigned to the idea since I haven't written on my novel in a while and I want to make sure I continue writing on it.

As I tidied my desk and sat before my typewriter my ideas started flowing, as they do every time I sit in front of a typewriter or have a quill in hand.

***

'What do you mean the Kingdom is in
disarray?' I asked my father who had
just entered my chambers.

'The other King has stuck one of our
towns on the borders, they believe he
is starting a war with us' my father
replied, annoyed at my questioning
him.

'But why? We haven't done anything to
offend him'

'He is a ruthless King who will stop
at nothing to get what he wants,
Julieanne. Be careful with how you
and your husband handle this and be
aware that the Former King and I will
be assisting in the decision making
since we have been doing this for much
longer than you and your husband'

'I understand that and appreciate it. Maybe if we find out what he is after then he will back off?'

'That would achieve nothing, if we send anyone to him, they will kill them'

'How do you know that?'

'Because the King has done this before, and we did exactly that. 12 of our men were slaughtered that day'

'If he has attacked us previously, why not stop him before?'

'Because he is a strong force'

'But we have the most trained soldier and the most equipment and training to win the battle, if we were to have one'

'And risk losing innocent lives? We sent him a treaty agreement to encourage him to stop the war before his whole kingdom was slaughtered. He took that kindly and backed off'

'Surely, you did more than just write out a treaty agreement. What did you give him?'

'That does not matter, all that does is that it worked, and we saved most of our people'

''most'?' I questioned.

'Yes, those that were lost working out what the King wanted and Eliza—' he cut himself off before continuing 'It doesn't matter, all that matters now is how to stop him again'

'Who is Eliza?'

'She is no one you need to concern yourself with'

'*Who is she?*' I demanded.

'Do not use that tone with me young lady, you may be Queen but I am still your father'

'True, but like you said, I am the *Queen*. To disobey me would be treason. Do you really want to deal with treason charges?'

'Fine, but watch your threats. *Elizabeth* was a young maiden that we traded alongside our treaty agreement. The King was looking for a bride at the time, and decided he wanted someone beautiful and fair from our kingdom'

'You *Traded* someone into a marriage treaty? Did she even want to go?'

'No, of course she didn't. She also happened to be a cousin of your husband, but the King wanted someone of royal blood. And knowing that we would not send out Princesses or Princes to him, we resorted to Elizabeth'

'How could you do that? She would have had a happy life here! And you sent her away to marry a ruthless King? What is wrong with you!'

'Julieanne! That is enough!' he snapped 'Now if you don't mind, I am going to arrange a meeting about what we are going to do about this war threat. You are more than welcome to join, *My Queen*' he growled the last words to the sentence, as if to scare me in some way.

'I will. That way you will not be able to *Trade* any of our people' I growled back.

***

'Emma?! Why are you sleeping at your desk?!' questioned Ma when she stormed into my room the following morning.

'Maa! I'm trying to sleep!' I whined as Ma opened my blinds letting all of the sun shine on my face. 'Why did you have to open the blinds!' I continued.

'You need to wake up and get ready, it's 6:40, we need to go and sign the paperwork otherwise we will miss our appointment. I believe Brendan collected his paperwork early this morning to get his Ma to sign as she is on bed rest, he will be meeting us down there

'Bed rest? Why?' I jerked my head up and looked directly into her kind, brown eyes.

'She is unwell, that is all I have been told. Perhaps you should be talking about this to Brendan?'

'I've asked, but he insists on getting the wedding stuff out of the way first'

'Well, let's do exactly that' she leaned down and pressed a kiss to my forehead before continuing 'I am sure she will be fine'

'Yeah, I hope so...' I replied, solemnly.

'Right! Get ready! We cannot be late!' she stressed before leaving the room, giving me a chance to finally wake up.

Once I had finished dressing into my favourite outfit and went downstairs to make a quick coffee before heading off to sign my wedding permission.

'Are you making coffee!?' Ma called from her room.

'Yes, Ma!' I replied, 'Would you like one?!' I asked.

'Yes, thank you!' she replied.

How hard can this wedding thing really be? I mean, just say 'I do' and the problem is solved. I suppose the moving house part and sharing everything will be a challenging thing, but I am sure Brendan and I will be able to work it out. But the bigger question yet, is what's going on with his Ma? I mean she has been inside her house for weeks now, and I haven't seen her in town. And given the size of our town, I see just about everyone. This means she won't leave her house, and she is on bed rest. But for how long has she been? Is that what Brendan was holding back the other day? If so, why? —

'Emma, what are you thinking about? You are going to let your coffee go cold' Ma interrupted and began sipping her coffee.

'Sorry Ma, I was just thinking about the wedding and Brendan's Ma. Shouldn't she be at the wedding?' I asked, feeling guilty about having a wedding when she was unable to attend.

'Of course, she should, but in saying that, if you don't marry Brendan before Friday then you will need to marry Kyle, I am sure Brendan's Ma understands what is going on and why we are unable to delay the wedding'

'It just seems unfair...'

'All of this is unfair, but that is a part of life'

'Yeah, I guess it is'

As Ma and I finished our coffee and headed to the wedding officials office I began to feel nauseous. *It's probably just from the nerves.* I thought to myself, hoping to make myself feel better.

My nerves began to settle a little bit as we approached the building and I saw Brendan standing in front. Knowing that he will be here also makes it all the much better.

'Hey Em, Mrs Hicks,' Brendan acknowledges as we arrive at the doors.

'Hey,' Ma and I said in unison.

'Are you ready?' asked Brendan, looking directly at me, probably to get an understanding of whether or not I am sure that I want to go through with the wedding.

I nodded once 'Yes, let's get this done...' I replied with more certainty than I expected to hear in my voice.

'Ok...' he replied with a small, encouraging smile. I returned his encouraging smile with my own before turning a heading into the building, ready to sign all the required paperwork to allow Brendan and I to marry.

Once we arrived inside, the receptionist looked at us and said that she would grab the paperwork and the wedding official. Since he needs to be a witness to the signing of the papers. Brendan's Ma was an exception, I guess.

'Sign here and here' the official directed, pointing to the areas that required our signatures. 'Be aware that this is an official document in which you cannot change your mind. Once you sign it there is no going back' he continued dryly.

'Thank you' Brendan and I replied in unison.

The signing lasted about 5 more minutes after we signed it, the official wanted to give us all of the required information and for us to select a day on which the wedding would take place. We selected Thursday, which is two days away. Plenty of time to prepare for the wedding.

On the way out from the signing, Ma stated 'Are you too going to talk about this?'

'Yes, did you want to go for a walk?' I asked Brendan.

'To the fields? It's private and quiet' he replied with a question of his own.

'Yes, that would be perfect,' I smiled.

'Good,' he replied with a smile of his own before returning to Ma 'Mrs. Hicks, I will have her returned shortly. Don't worry, the wedding will be perfect' he smiled at Ma.

'Thank you, Brendan' she replied before turning and heading towards the house. Leaving Brendan and I to head to the fields and begin our talk of our future.

***

'Are you nervous about the wedding?' I asked Brendan and I snuggled into him as we sat and watched the clouds move across the open sky.

'Yes, are you?' he questioned.

'Yes, but it should be ok, right? Especially since it will only be yourself, Ma, and I in attendance and we don't need to make love speeches or anything' I thought aloud 'But even if we did it would be ok...right?'

'Yes, it would be' he spoke as he gently pushed me back so I was lying on the cool grass 'It will be perfect because you are my bride' he continued before placing a blissfully soft kiss on my lips.

'And you will be my groom' I said between kisses 'Do you think we will be ok?' I asked, pulling anyway enough to look into his passionate eyes.

'I know we will,' he replied with a smirk before laying on his back, so he was also able to see the clouds passing above us.

We lay there in silence for what felt like forever, delaying the inevitable conversations that we needed to have with each other. But the silence was nice, comforting even. With our lives being turned upside down, we rarely get a peaceful moment together.

'So...how do you think Kyle will react when word gets out about our wedding?'

'I think he will be furious, and not to mention his Pa, who will be even more furious that Kyle failed at getting me to marry him'

'Oh, yeah. I didn't even think of that'

'And that is why I am the brains and your looks' I laughed.

'You are definitely the looks and the brains, I'm the witty sidekick' he laughed.

'Sidekick?' I laughed even harder.

I love these calm and peaceful moments that Brendan and I share, it is purely magical. I thought as I stared at the sky.

'That cloud looks like a dog' I say, interrupting the silence that eloped us.

'Haha, yeah it does. That one looks like a snake'

'Or a worm'

'True, it could also be a caterpillar'

'Indeed' I replied before continuing to say, 'There's an elephant there'

'I don't see it...' Brendan replies as he turns his hand into different angles trying to get a better angle.

'There' I replied, pointing towards where it was 'There are the ears, and there's the trunk and there is the head' I elaborated after he gave me a questionable look, still unsure of where it was.

'Nope, still don't see it' he laughed.

I don't know how long we just laid there looking up at the clouds and laughing about what we could and could not see, but it was all worth it

CHAPTER FIFTEEN

As I nervously paced around my room, I felt my nerves growing as the clock ticked closer and closer to noon. The time that I will become Mrs. Smith.

The summer heat made me sweat as I paced the room. The fans do not seem to be working at all.

Why did the wedding have to be in the middle of summer? Why not autumn when the weather is cooling down ready for winter? I thought as I continued pacing.

Yesterday was spent going over all of the details and what I would wear, Ma managed to find her old wedding dress and it fit me perfectly. Planning for the wedding made me nervous, even thinking about it. But today is different, I am nervous to be married, to agree to it. I haven't seen Brendan since the day we signed the papers. He had been busy with his Ma and the tasks that Ma gave him after he dropped me home from the fields. Ma was always prepared, even if it was short notice. However, I wouldn't be surprised if she already had all of the information ready for when I or Maybelle did marry.

I obviously made Maybelle my flower girl and ring bearer. Ma was my maid of honor, and I refused to let anyone else but her walk me down the aisle, even if there will definitely be a backlash to it. Brendan got one of his friends to attend and be his ring bearer and support person. Everything was set to go, the wedding officials called this morning to confirm the wedding agreement was still taking place, and to confirm the time, Ma answered the telephone for me as I had been stressing too much to think clearly.

I am continuously coming to the same conclusions in my mind 'What if I stuff it up?', 'What if Brendan changed his mind?', 'When am I going to move out?'. All of these questions circulated. I told Ma about them and she said that they were normal and that everyone thinks about them on their wedding day, then she told me to rest up.

I am yet to rest, so I came straight up here and started to pace my room. I am far too excited and nervous to rest and I cannot think straight enough to read or write, so the only other thing I could think about is pacing.

I mean surely I won't fail at my own wedding? I asked myself as Maybelle flew into my room with her beautiful dress and hairstyle.

'Maybelle, you look amazing!' I exclaimed 'You look good enough to be the bride!'

'Yes, well, I'm not as stunning as you are, Emma' she replied 'Have you even rested? All I can hear is your footsteps' she continued.

'No, I don't think I'd be able to stay still long enough, haha' I laughed.

'Well, stop worrying! It is all going to be perfect and you and Brendan are perfect together! So, there is absolutely nothing to be worried about'

'Look at you, sounding all grown up'

She smiles before asking 'So, how are you feeling?'

'Like I am about to throw up'

'Well, please don't. Or at least not on me. That would be wonderful' she joked, causing me to laugh a little.

'Maybelle? Emma?' Ma called before arriving in my doorway 'Everything ok?' she continued.

'Yes, Ma' replied Maybelle, 'Emma is feeling like she will throw up though' she continued.

'Well, she won't, it is just nerves. You will be fine, Emma, dear. So, stop worrying...ok?' she asked.

'A little easier said than done, Ma. And you have both already told me that" I replied.

'Yes, indeed it is. But it is doable. And if we *both* have told you then maybe you should follow our advice?' she replied.

'I am trying...but it is hard" I replied with a small frown. Maybell, sensing my sadness came over and placed her arms around my waist, making me feel safe, loved, and wanted. Her hugs always meant the world to me, especially since she doesn't hug me often.

Once Maybelle released me from her hug, Ma ushered me out of the room and asked her to boil the kettle and make me some relaxing tea. My own recipe. Before turning around to face me.

'Emma, trust me, I know this is daunting. But it will all be worth it. You are going to make an amazing bride, wife, mother, aunty, and whatever else comes next. I believe in you and I believe that you will get everything that you want. You are a hard worker, therefore, you are able to do anything, and your determination is a beautiful force to be reckoned with. So, don't let your fears get the better of you. Enjoy your wedding day, it will only happen once. And you and Brendan truly are made for each other' she stated.

'Thank you, Ma. But I don't think all of that is true. I've taken the next two days off work, are you sure you will be fine working and getting more money for the family? I can return to work after the wedding?' I replied.

Sighing she replied 'No, don't do that. We will be completely fine. Stop worrying about us. If we need you, I will call or something'

'Thank you,' I replied.

Once Ma had left the room once again, I felt my fears and insecurities settle in once again. Forcing me to rethink my life choices. But like Ma has stated the wedding will be fine, just need to get through it, and Brendan and I will be completely and utterly fine...I hope.

***

'Emma, darling. Please remember to smile as we walk down the aisle, otherwise, you will look like a bride who is grim about her own wedding. Something we both don't want' Ma informs before looping her arm through mine, preparing me for the walk down the aisle, to my future husband, Brendan Smith.

As the music began to play, I felt terrified, excited, nervous but also joyful. But as soon as I began to walk, needing Ma to gently pull me to set my walking into motion, I felt pure fear. But like Ma announced on the way down here, mask your fear with a smile.

I don't remember the aisle being this long before...it seems to be going on forever. I thought as I started walking down the aisle.

I finally had the nerve to look at Brendan, and as soon as my eyes met his I felt all of my worries and fears disappear into nothingness. I couldn't help but wonder if that was all I needed to do to make my fears and worries disappear earlier.

Brendan looked breathtaking, I am assuming he borrowed the deluxe suit from the town's wedding and special occasions shop, suited for all events. It matched him perfectly and the black matched his eye. I don't think I have ever seen him so perfect in my life.

What felt like forever, I finally made it to the end of the aisle and Brendan's hand was already stretched out to hold mine, tentatively, I took it and smiled at him before whispering *'Hey'*.

'Hey,' he whispered back.

As the wedding official read out the wedding vows, I found myself blocking out everything except Brendan and the way his eyes glistened in the sun. It was purely magical.

Since Brendan and I were doing our vows, due to the fact that we didn't have any time to write them. My attention snapped back to the wedding official when he asked Brendan if he would take me as his wife, and my attention refocused on Brendan, as if worried that he would say no.

'I do,' he announced with a goofy grin.

'Emma, do you take Brendan Smith to be your husband?' asked the wedding official.

'I do'

'You may now give each other your rings'

Our ring bearers stepped forward and handed our rings to us and we tentatively and carefully took turns putting the ring on each other.

'Mr and Mrs. Emma Smith, I now pronounce you husband and wife. You may now kiss the bride' the wedding official announced.

Before the wedding official even got the chance to finish his sentence Brendan had already hooked me by the waist and pulled me towards him, kissing me passionately. I don't know how long we stood there, arm in arm and kissing each other. Eventually, Brendan broke away and turned to face our friends and family, with the biggest grin on his face that I have ever seen.

Once the wedding was over, Ma had arranged for everyone to come over to our house for a BBQ. Which I thought was a great idea. On our way out of the church we were stopped by most of the townsfolk who came to wish us well.

Well, I guess the secret is out...now there is only a limited amount of time before Kyle and his Pa figure it all out and will come asking questions. But for now, I was to enjoy spending time with Brendan and my family. I thought as we began walking towards the house, Ma and Maybelle were walking ahead with some of our friends. Brendan and I stayed back, walking a little slower so we could both have a moment to pause.

'How are you feeling?' asked Brendan.

'I'm well, I'm glad we did get married. I wouldn't want to be married to anyone else' I replied smiling, 'And, B, don't worry we will figure everything out' I continued.

Brendan came to an abrupt halt as if realising something for the first time.

'Everything ok?' I asked as I turned to face him, looking into his beautiful, kind eyes.

'There is still so much that we need to do and I don't know how much time I have to get it all done, with Ma being ill and all,' he replied, sadly.

'We will work it all out. One step at a time. And your Ma will be better soon, I hope' I replied as I looped my arm through his and gently pulled him into motion so we were once again walking home.

After a small silence had settled between us, I wondered what was going on with B's Ma, but today was not the time nor the place to discuss it. We walked in silence, neither of us knew what to say, but B finally broke the silence and asked.

'How does it feel to be Mrs. Emma Smith?'

'Lovely, because it means I will be with you forever' I replied smiling, the warm glint in Brendan's eyes had returned, blocking the earlier sadness. I know it is still there, but he is trying to be positive.

'Indeed it does' he replied as we arrived at the house and headed inside.

Ma did a great job with the house, she has made all of the snacks herself and has decorated the house with streamers.

'Emma!' called Maybelle.

'Hey, Maybelle,' I replied.

'How are you feeling?' she asked as she flung her arms around me.

'Pretty good, glad it is over and done with' I shrugged.

'That is good, I think'

'It is'

'Maybelle, can you come and help with the BBQ!' called Ma from the backyard.

'Coming Ma' she called back and headed out to join her.

'Maybelle is a delight' Brendan pipped in once Maybelle had already left.

'She sure is,' I laughed.

As the day drew to an end, everything began to settle down, and most of our friends had left. Leaving Maybelle, Ma, Brendan and I sitting around the dining room table. Ma started telling us stories from her wedding and Maybelle was telling jokes. The night was truly magical.

CHAPTER SIXTEEN

Brendan ended up leaving late last night, not wanting to leave his Ma alone overnight, allowing me to spend some time with Ma and Maybelle. Maybelle had heaps of questions, some of which I could answer. But for others, Ma had to answer for me. Maybelle was fascinated by the whole wedding scene, but of course, I still don't know everything about weddings and since my wedding was extremely basic and unusual, I couldn't help answer them.

I had contacted Edwardson about making an article about forced marriages and he has told me that it is ok to write but to be mindful of what I say and how I say it.

Time to start writing. I thought as I sat at my desk.

A Woman's Right to a Happy Marriage

Everyone deserves the perfect, dream wedding with the partner that they love and elect to marry.

This applies to both genders, however, more so to females in our society.

I was recently challenged by a family in my town. The Son and his Pa had decided that I was to marry him, and since my Pa is no longer with us, therefore, I couldn't get him to refuse. In order to stop the marriage to a person I didn't love, I ended up approaching my partner and asking for his hand in marriage, I then needed to approach the town's wedding officials and get them to agree to the ceremony. This took about two days for us to convince the wedding officials to do it and we were required to sign paperwork stating that both our Ma's agreed and both parties agreed.

I was then married yesterday, to the person I wanted to marry. Our wedding was nothing fancy and we didn't have time to send invites out. This is something I cannot change, but if I could I would.

Every woman deserves to have their family present at their wedding. Every individual should have a support group there.

Thousands of women around the world are forced to marry a man they do not love or even know for that matter, some aren't even over 18 years of age before they are to be wed to a man 3 times their age. I understand that some cultures may do this for their own cultural beliefs. I firmly believe that individuals have the right to a marriage of love and happiness, not one of discomfort and regret. I also believe that the decision to be wed should be between the two individuals who are in love and not the parents, and it not be arranged by the parents or guardians.

While I understand that my opinion may offend some individuals, I am also aware that my opinion will empower others. Every personal opinion matters and every single voice deserves the chance to be heard. Especially females in today's society. No one deserves to be treated less than their male counterparts, and this includes marriage.

If you are unhappy in your marriage, seek help or a way out. Marriage is supposed to be a happy, joyous thing. Not one that you will grow to regret.

Stand up for yourself and seek happiness. Everyone deserves that much.

Written by,

Emma Hicks

There is so much more I can write on this article, however, due to the limited space I have in the newspaper, unfortunately, I am unable to continue writing on it. While this is disappointing, since I only touched base on the issues surrounding forced marriages, there is so much more that I have left unsaid.

There are so many things that I still have yet to say, but I will find a way to express my thoughts without repercussions and judgment. While this won't happen for quite some time, I believe that the time will come when people can speak freely without feeling like they are in the wrong and that they shouldn't be saying anything at all.

But for now, I will need to settle for small articles in the newspaper. Small, limited space in the article where I can express my thoughts on some issues but am judged on other things. I am more or less judged when I speak my mind on feminism, the rights of the individual, equal opportunities for both of our genders and lastly the equal pay rate between each gender. I am more inclined to write what I believe to be right, however, most of the time I have to write about things that I do not believe in or that I don't understand why people need to know about it.

'Emma!' called Ma as she marched into my room.

'Yes?' I called back.

'Why aren't you already up?' she asked.

'I am, I have been writing an article'

'Oh...ok. Well, have you spoken to Brendan since yester-day?'

'No, I will be contacting him shortly, I am going to invite him over for coffee. Has Kyle been over?'

'No, I went in town earlier, and I heard some of the towns-folk saying that he and his Pa have left town once they heard about your wedding'

'Oh, that would be wonderful' I spoke as I rose and headed for the door, heading for the telephone 'I hope they don't come back, as all they will do is cause more trouble'

'Yes, they will. Are you and Brendan going to move in together'

'We will, not sure when though'

'Well, if Kyle and his Pa are moving out of town, their property would be going up for sale soon'

'Indeed it will be. I am yet to discuss it with Brendan, I am hoping to talk more this afternoon' I replied before excusing myself to call Brendan.

As the telephone rang, I caught myself thinking about everything that had happened over the past months, how much my life had changed, for better and for worse. First, Ben leaves town. Then Pa dies in the mining accident. And my tea business brought in way more money than originally planned. I was being forced into a marriage I didn't want and was able to get out of it and marry Brendan. And now I am expected to move in with him and have children.

'Hello?' Brendan answered.

'Hey B, it's Emma' I replied, smiling. His voice calmed my racing thoughts.

'Did you get much sleep?' he asked, he sounded tired.

'Yes, did you?'

'No, not really. Ma was up all night throwing up, so I was helping her'

'Oh, that's horrible'

'Yes, it is. Did you need something?'

'I was wondering if you wanted to come for coffee?'

'Yes, that would be wonderful. We have lots to discuss'

'Great, I'll see you soon,' I replied before hanging up.

'Is he coming over?' Ma asked when I got to the living room.

'Yes, he will be over shortly' I replied as I sat in my chair.

'Well, I am going to head over to Penny's house for lunch, I will give you some privacy'

'Thank you, Ma'

With Maybelle already at school and Ma going to her friend's house, Brendan and I will finally be able to have the conversation that both of us have been putting off for the last couple of months. And I know we both have a lot to talk about.

***

After letting Brendan in, I headed for the kitchen to make our coffee, I have a feeling we are both going to need it.

'Where is Mrs. Hicks?' Brendan asked from the living room.

'She has gone over to Penny's for lunch' I replied as I headed for the living room with the coffee.

Brendan thanked me as I handed him his coffee. And I headed for my chair, ready to have the conversation of our lives.

'So, where did you want to start?' I asked, being just us we don't need to hold back anything that is on our minds.

'Honestly, I am not too sure'

'Ok...well, let's start simple. Do you want to move in together?'

'Of course, I do. But I can't at the moment. Not until Ma is feeling better'

'That's ok, hopefully, she will be soon'

'No, I don't think she will be,' he replied with a sad, pained smile.

'Why? What's wrong?' I asked, and I couldn't even mask the concern in my voice.

'You have to promise not to tell anyone...ok?'

'Ok...'

'I don't know the best way to tell you, I haven't said it was allowed yet. But I think if I just say it outright, it might make it easier...' he replied, sensing his discomfort, I moved so I was sitting with him and took his hand in mine.

'What's going on, B?' I asked again, softly.

'*Ma has cancer*' he whispered, barely audible, as soon as the words left his mouth his whole body sagged and leaned into me, and the tears began streaming down his face like small, sad waterfalls.

'Oh, B!' I exclaimed, 'Why didn't you tell me sooner?' I asked softly as I held him in my arms.

We stayed like that until B was able to regain his composure. I don't think I have ever seen him this distraught over anything before. But this is something that warrants it.

'Is there anything I can do to help?' I asked quietly.

'No...' he replied.

'Let me know if you do...ok?'

'Ok...' he started before adding, *'But you can't tell anyone, Ma doesn't want the town to know, she doesn't want pity and for people to think even less of her'*

'I promise'

Seeing Brendan like this is killing me, and there is nothing I can say or do to change what is happening to his Ma. I guess, to some extent, it was a good idea not to tell me until

after the wedding, otherwise, I don't know how I would
have reacted.

'Em?' he said.

'Yes?'

'I love you' he replied, finally looking up at me. Tears glistened in his eyes, but there was nothing but honesty shown
in them.

'I love you too, B'

After a long pause, Brendan reluctantly rose off me
grabbed his coffee, and started to sip at it. *I wonder what
he is thinking.* I thought curiously.

'You know, Em. If Ma died, I would inherit the house, so
we could just move in there' he spoke, more confidently
than before, but the lingering sadness stayed, dominating
his usual kind voice.

'I know that, but you don't know that she is going to die,
she could fight it and win'

'Has anyone in these towns ever won against cancer?' he asked, sadly.

'No...but your Ma is strong. She will get through this' I spoke, with more certainty than I thought I had in me.

'I hope so...' he spoke, calmly, 'How did you move forward after your Pa died?'

'It took a while for me to realize that he wouldn't want me to be miserable all of the time, that he would have wanted me to be happy and continue to write. I am not over him, but I have moved past grief and I am now seeing all of the wonderful things he did for our family and the town. I miss him dreadfully every day, and I am continually reminded that he won't be coming home, but I know that he is still with us'

'That sounds nice, do you think I will ever let myself be forgiven for not preventing her death?'

'B, there is nothing you can do to prevent her death, and that is the same with my Pa. He was determined to work in the mines, to get money for our family, but also to ensure that everybody was safe and knew what they were doing. He cared too much about the townsfolk and the people from the other towns to let them go in alone, even if they didn't need him. And the mines are never a safe place to work. And now with the new mines up and running a lot of the men are returning to the mines, as most feel obligated to do so'

'So, you and your family were trying to convince him to leave the mines?'

'Yes, the day before it collapsed. I was the only one who didn't want him to leave, he loved working in the mines, and he loved helping people. I wouldn't want to take that away from him, especially when it is one of the only things that made him smile, besides our family of course'

'I don't know what I am going to do when Ma dies...'

'You are going to be strong and we will get through it together, just like how you supported me through Pa's death. I will do the same for you, always'

'Thank you, Em'

I wish I could convince him that everything will be ok, but I cannot prevent death and I don't know what is going to happen or how he will react. But I do know that he needs me, so I am going to do whatever it takes to ensure I am there to support him. I thought to myself before B interrupted me.

'Ok, now that you know about Ma. How about we discuss something else?' B questioned.

'What else would you like to address?' I asked, curiously.

'What about the fact that Kyle and his Pa left town shortly after our wedding?'

'Yeah, I did hear about that earlier from Ma. Do you think that they left out of shame or embarrassment since I refused to marry Kyle?'

'That is very likely the case, however, I don't believe it. But some of the townsfolk are saying that they will be returning, they have just left town until the marriage excitement has passed, but I don't think they will be coming back anytime soon'

'Good, they shouldn't. They would only cause more problems'

'That's true, I don't want them to come back either'

'Well, I best be heading off, I am sure Ma needs help' announces Brendan as he rises and places a sweet, loving kiss on my lips. 'But I will see you tomorrow, my beautiful wife'

'I can't wait' I smile against his lips before kissing him again.

I walked him to the door and we hugged for a while and bid each other farewell until tomorrow.

Chapter Seventeen

It has been a week since my wedding ceremony. Brendan has been with his Ma for most of the time, as she is rapidly losing to cancer, and it is absolutely heartbreaking. I visited her yesterday, and I didn't even have the courage to stay the whole time. I spent about an hour with them before Brendan walked me home. I wish I had the courage to stay longer, but it was breaking my heart seeing her like that. Ma had stopped by a couple of days ago to give her some assistance while Brendan and I could talk some things over.

As I sat patiently in the living room, waiting for Maybelle to return home from school, Ma entered the room looking worried.

'What's wrong?' I asked, rising from my chair and standing before her.

'It's Clara–'

As soon as her name came off Ma's lips I bolted for the door, Ma following closely behind, rushing to get to Brendan's house.

It only took 5 minutes to get to Brendan's house, but when we arrived, the air chilled. Death lingered around the house, waiting impatiently to take Clara away from Brendan.

I stormed into the house to find Brendan kneeling by his Ma's bed, he glanced up at me with pure sadness in his eye.

I gave him a small, sad smile as I knelt down before him and held Clara's hand within my own. She looked as white as snow and I could feel her warmth slowly leaving her body.

I could hear Ma gasp from behind me as she entered the room, I'd lost her in my panic about getting here. She was out of breath, but she managed to kneel beside the bed, alongside Brendan and I as we spent Clara's remaining breaths with her. Brendan shouldn't have to do this alone, and since she was like a second Ma to me, I'd made sure I came when Brendan asked.

I knew Clara's soul had left her body the minute the air chilled more, and in that moment, I felt time freeze. I glanced over at Brendan and took his hand in mine as I watched the silent tears fall down his face. Ma grabbed his other hand and helped me lift him to his feet. He can't stay here, the town's medic will be here shortly. As soon as Brendan and I went outside, Brendan collapsed to the ground in sobs. Ma had left us to go and telephone the medic, so I was left to help Brendan. There is nothing worse than losing a parent, but in the last year, Brendan had lost two.

'Brendan?' I whispered into his ear *'I am so sorry'* I continued. I didn't really know what else to say to comfort him.

'Emma?' Ma gently touched my arm as she spoke my name, I didn't even hear her come over.

'Yes?' I asked, once I reluctantly stood and walked away from my husband who was crumpled up on the grass.

'You need to take Brendan somewhere else, perhaps our house? Make him some tea or coffee. He will be staying with us for a while until he feels a little better. Then we will work out what to do from there. But he cannot stay here. The medic will be arriving soon, and I think it is best if Brendan isn't here when he does arrive' she explained quietly, even though I know Brendan isn't listening to what we are saying, I understand why Ma spoke quietly.

'Ok...will you be staying here?'

'Yes, I'll be home once I have everything here sorted out'

'Ok,' I replied as I turned back towards my husband and spoke gently, *'B...can you stand for me?'*

Slowly, he rose with me. I was supporting most of his weight.

'I...ca...can't...lea...ve...her....here' He spoke between sobs.

'I know, but we need to...Ma will be here with her the whole time. There is nothing for you to worry about,' I spoke sternly, but softly before continuing *'And there's nothing you can do here'*

'O...ok' he agreed reluctantly as I walked slowly back home with him.

Once we arrived home, I took Brendan to the living room and sat him down before going and making some of my soothing tea. Hopefully, it will calm him down a bit. After the tea was ready, I handed B his mug and placed mine on the small table in the center of the room.

'Are you cold?' I asked softly.

'A little' he replied.

His initial shock seemed to have worn out. That's got to be something. I thought as I lit the fire.

'Em...?' spoke Brendan, barely whispering. I am surprised I heard him over the crackling of the fire starting.

'Yeah?'

'I feel empty,' he replied.

'I know...but it gets easier'

'I don't know about that'

'Trust me'

'Ok...'

Not long after Brendan fell asleep in my arms, with the warmth from the fire heating the chilled air. He looked peaceful, but the bags under his eyes held the story of the struggle his life had been through over the last couple of months.

I don't know how long I stayed there, cradling my husband, but I could hear Ma and Maybelle arriving home- Ma had sent Maybelle over to her friend's place until she came to collect her. Maybelle didn't mind.

Once they came into view, I put my finger to my mouth. A silent plea for them to be quiet, so they don't wake up Brendan. I rose and headed to meet them in the kitchen.

'What happened?' I asked after Ma asked Maybelle to get ready for bed.

'The medic signed some forms, announcing Clara's official death. Then he got his small team over to transport her to the graves. Brendan will be expected to arrange the funeral which is to take place no longer than two weeks from now...do you think he can handle it?'

'I am his wife, therefore, it also falls on me to arrange. I will do what I can where I can. But obviously, he is the only one who can sign all of the paperwork. But we should be ok...I will ask for help if needed'

'How was he this afternoon?'

'Devastated. He fell asleep a while ago, I didn't want to wake him. He looks more peaceful now, less panicked'

'Yes, indeed he does. I know this might be too soon to mention. But as soon as the funeral is sorted out and done. Brendan will need to decide if you both are moving into the house or if he is selling. If you decide to move into the house, I will help where I can to move your stuff in and clean the place up'

'Thank you, Ma' I replied with a sad smile before returning to my spot in the lounge next to B.

***

'Is there anything you need help with?' I asked Brendan as we sat around the dining room table, planning the funeral.

It has been nearly a week since Clara died, and Brendan is slowly accepting it. But planning the funeral has been difficult. He tried doing it yesterday, but he couldn't focus.

And I, unfortunately, needed to write an article announcing her death to the town, and that needed to include the time and day of the funeral. Brendan had decided earlier that he wanted the funeral to be next Tuesday, giving me plenty of time to write and publish the paper before the funeral.

'Is there anything you wanted me to include in the article?'

'You can include anything you wish, Em,' he replied with a sad smile.

'Ok...' I spoke uncertainty, before rising and heading to my room to write the article. I hated leaving Brendan alone to go over everything, but I needed to get this article written.

I hate writing about death, it's depressing. But I hate it even more when it is someone that I care about. All of the deaths in town, I am required to write about and give out the dates of the funeral. Obviously, this death and the funeral preparations have taken a little longer for me to figure out since I do not want to rush Brendan on any of it.

'Right, how hard can this be?' I asked myself quietly as I sat down at my desk, preparing to write about the death of a mother figure- Clara.

Celebration of Life

On Monday 18th of July, we mourn the loss of a prominent figure in our town, Clara Smith.

Clara Smith was and always will be a respected part of this community.

As the townsfolk are all aware, The Smith Family has had a year and a half, with the only remaining member in town being Brendan Smith. With Brendan's Pa leaving town and remarrying, and now the loss of Mrs. Clara Smith, the family is left devastated.

For those who are unaware, Brendan and I had just gotten married the day before Clara passed. This affected both Brendan's and my own family's lives, as well as many other families within this town.

Brendan and I have now planning the funeral over the past couple of days, we have arrived at the funeral on Tuesday, the 26th at 10 AM. The funeral is open to everyone in town, everyone is welcome to attend and say their farewells.

Please if you are finding Brendan to give him well wishes, he will be staying with my family until he has figured out what he wants to do.

Clara was one of the best nurses in our town, she saved so many people's lives and lived a great life which she loved. She loved this town, the people, her family and friends as well as medicine. She lived to help people.

Please attend the funeral if you are able to.

Written by:

Emma Hicks/Smith

***

'Emma, it's so good to see you!' exclaimed Edwardson as I walked into the Newspaper office.

'Hello, Ed. How are you?' I asked as I placed the story on his desk. I prefer to hand in the Celebrations of Life in person.

'I'm well, how are you handling the death of Clara?'

'I'm getting there'

'And Brendan?'

'As expected, but he is slowly getting there'

'That's good to hear' he spoke as he flipped through the article. Sadness etched into his face.

'Yeah, it is,' I said, sadly 'What do you think?' I continued.

'This is beautiful, I'll have it posted for this afternoon's newspaper release. I will be attending the funeral too. Do you need numbers?'

'I am not too sure yet, Brendan and I are still arranging and going over all of that. But most likely, no, since I am hoping to have the ceremony outside. I just have to get Brendan to agree on the idea'

'That sounds like a plan then, I wish you luck' he smiled.

'Thank you' Returning his smile, I headed for the door.

I have always loved this town, the views, and the country-side, it creates the best sunrises and sunsets. The perfect place for weddings and photos. The people of the town are lovely too, granted, we do have a couple of cranky townsfolk, but they generally stick to themselves.

As I am walking through my town, everyone is smiling as I pass them. Creating a warm feeling inside me, a feeling of pure friendliness and hope. The townsfolk support each other when things are both good and bad. Currently, the news about Clara's passing hasn't spread due to the fact that Ma asked the doctors to keep it to themselves until I officially announce it through the paper. I told Edwardson yesterday morning, informing him of Clara's death that I will be dropping down the article for the paper's release tomorrow. He insisted that he got another writer to write the article, but I insisted it would be okay and that I should be the one to write it since I knew Clara so well. He reluctantly agreed, but he wasn't thrilled with the idea. But I think he figured out that I wasn't not going to write the article, and rather than upsetting me, he'd just agreed to let me write it. And I am thankful for that.

***

The day of Clara's funeral had finally arrived, after nights of watching Brendan panic over the arrangements, I will be glad for it to be over. Brendan needs to say his goodbyes so he can begin to heal.

The ceremony turned out to be quite large, with most of the townsfolk attending. Thankfully, Brendan had agreed to have the ceremony outside, which allowed us to have any number of guests.

After the official speeches were done, Brendan and I said our farewells and then floated around the guests. After about half an hour, Brendan looked ready to head home, so I told Ma and Maybelle that we would be heading out and to let others know. Brendan handled the funeral much better than I expected him to, I expected him to shut down completely. But I think he soon realized that funerals are a chance for people to say goodbye and tell stories from the life that Clara had. This in itself made Brendan relax, ever so slightly.

As soon as Brendan's head hit his pillow that night, he was fast asleep. And he finally looked at peace for the first time today.

Chapter Eighteen

'Emma? Where did your Ma put the sugar?' called B from the kitchen.

'It should be in the top left cupboard above the stove!' I called back from my small office.

It has now been three months since Clara died, we had eventually moved into their family house just last month. Brendan didn't want to move in quickly and we had to pack up some of Clara's items. They are now in storage, Brendan, understandably, refusing to throw any of it out. The house is much more spacious than my own family house. I even had enough space to fit in a small office in which I do most of my writing. I am currently only writing a small amount of articles, due to the simple fact that I took a couple of weeks off to support Brendan on more than one occasion and I took more time off when we were moving out. Thankfully, Edwardson was more supportive of my requests and allowed me to take the time off and resume work when I was ready to do so.

'How's the article coming along? Is this the big one that you are writing for the national paper?' Brendan asked, coming up behind me with two coffees in his hand. I gratefully took mine before answering.

'Yes, I have three weeks to submit. This will be the main article that I will be writing. Ed has said that he will not be giving me any more articles until I have completed my voluntary article. Especially since the national paper isn't happy about me writing about any of my thoughts, and this article is going to make a lot of people unhappy, but these things need to be said' I replied before taking a sip of the blissful coffee in my hand, the aroma filling the study almost instantly when B entered the room.

'That sounds stressful' he started, pausing to kiss my head, 'But I will need to head off to work myself, so, my love, I will see you this afternoon' he continued before placing a soft, delicate kiss on my lips.

'Ok...' I replied as I kissed him again. 'Be safe' I called before he'd left the room.

I hate that he is being forced to work in the mines, especially, after the last mine collapsed. I cannot lose him too. I thought to myself as I began to focus back on my article.

I have been staring blankly at my typewriter for about an hour, dwelling on the article title.

The Ideology of the Prejudice World We Live in

For as long as remember our society has been using prejudiced ideologies to shape and mold the way we think and act.

The preconceived, stereotypical opinions and ideologies are forcing the children and teenagers of this generation to be forced into doing things that they have no interest in doing or are frowned upon when they even attempt to try and achieve their goals.

I am a female novelist and I am being pushed aside to make room for male novelists, as the male sex is given the more dominant, superior position in society, whereas, women are expected to sit back and watch this happen. They are expected to stay at home, be a housewife, bear children, and tend to their husbands' and children's every need, they are rarely given the opportunities to work.

I am one of the few lucky ones in today's society, I am given the chance to express my thoughts through my local town's newspaper, and I am given the chance to make something of myself. While I am writing this article with the national newspaper pleading with me to not publish it, I am doing so with the knowledge that this article is going to give me both negative and positive responses. I am proud to be writing this article and I think that everything in this article is what both sexes deserve and what I believe to be fair and just.

For those that have not read my previous articles, my name is Mrs. Emma Smith, I recently married my husband, previously I was known as Emma Hicks.

I live in a small rural town in Newcastle, New South Wales called Kingship Valley. I am 19 years old. I have been writing for my local newspaper since I was 14, and have released over 100 articles in that period. Around half of them are about the rights and opportunities that both sexes should be able to obtain. However, this is my first nationally recognised, feminist article. I am proud to be writing it.

I have a sister named Maybelle, and my Ma. My Pa died in a mining accident late last year. This event was one of the first news articles that I have written for the national newspaper. As some of you may be aware, the national newspaper cannot stop smaller publishing newspaper houses from posting their articles in their papers, since they are expected to have 1 article from each publishing house. Therefore, this article has no option but to be present in the newspaper.

'Knock, knock?' spoke a voice from the doorway, startling me. I didn't even hear them enter the house but as soon as I heard his voice, I knew who it was.

'Ben!' I cried out as I jumped out of my chair and flung myself into his strong, reassuring arms. As soon as my body smacked against his, he instantly lifted me off the ground and spun around with me.

'Hey Emma' he replied as he placed my feet back onto the ground. But didn't release his hold on my waist.

'What are you doing here!? Did you send a telegram that I missed?' I couldn't think, as my mind was racing, but I didn't remember him sending word of his arrival.

'No, I thought I might come and surprise my superstar best friend' he replied, casually. I laughed before continuing.

'I haven't seen you in forever!' I exclaimed. 'Did you want coffee?' I asked before he could even react to my first question. And I stood out of his embrace and headed for the kitchen.

'You know, I was only here two months ago?'

'Well, it feels like longer than that since I saw you'

Once the coffee was made I handed Ben his mug and headed for the living room, once we were both settled in Ben asked.

'You know that article you wrote about the mining incident last year?'

'Of course, why?'

'I forgot to tell you, but that caused a lot of talk in my office building. Everyone was shocked that you wrote it and because of what the article was about'

'I would believe that. I received heaps of telegrams daily'

'I ran into Edwardson on my way through the town, and he informed me that you have quite a large, powerful article in motion?'

'Yes, that's correct. My biggest one yet. I have two weeks before submission and it is going into the national newspaper'

'What is this one going to be about?'

'Equal rights, gender equality and a bit more'

'So, you're writing an article that the national newspaper wouldn't want you to publish, and in publishing, you are doing so knowing that this will receive more backlash than your previously recognised national article...correct?'

'Yes, I am well aware of what is going to happen once I publish this article. But everything in the article needs to be heard, and it needs to be said. Otherwise, how are we expected to change the way society thinks and acts if we are all too afraid to speak up for what we believe in?'

'You make some good points, but be careful about what you write about. One misused word and your writing career will be over before it has begun' he warned as the front door opened, announcing Brendan's return home.

'Hey Ben,' he spoke as he walked over to me and kissed me softly on the lips, 'Em' he continued.

'Hey, Brendan,' Ben replied.

'I didn't know you were coming' Brendan replied as he sat next to me, enveloping me with his strong, protective arms falling casually over my body.

'Don't worry, neither did I' I replied to him and I leaned my head against his chest.

'Nothing beats a surprise visit, especially, if it is going to make Emma even more excited to see me'

'That's true,' I replied.

'So, where will you be staying?' asked Brendan.

'I was hoping to stay here, if not then I will stay in the small inn'

'You are more than welcome to stay here' I said.

'Thank you, Emma'

I am so thankful that both Brendan and Ben are also really close friends, I wouldn't want Brendan to feel uncomfortable in his own home, that wouldn't have been fair on him. Besides, we have a spare room that we have made up for when guests stay over, although, I'm pretty sure Maybelle has claimed it as her room since she is over here so often.

'That spare room is made up' I spoke, breaking the comfortable silence that fell over us.

'Don't you mean Maybelle's second room?' asked Brendan.

'Well, yes. But it isn't technically hers. She is just over here a lot and she stays in that room, so she has kind of claimed it as hers' I reassured Ben.

'That's fine by me, as long as Maybelle isn't going to kick me out,' he laughed.

'I think you might be safe'

***

'Do you mind that Ben is staying with us?' I asked Brendan as we lay in bed, snuggled against each other.

'I am fine with it, as long as it makes you happy' he replied with a smile.

'Yeah, it does, I like seeing him. He makes everything fun'

'And I don't' he asked, sarcastically.

'Of course, you do,' I replied smiling. 'But it's different,' I continued, cautious.

'Because I am your husband?'

'Partially, but also because we are a different sort of fun and I love you in a different way than I do Ben'

'That makes complete sense, but just so you know, I love you more' he replied before he kissed me passionately, daring me.

The following morning, I felt refreshed. Ready to begin the new day, I have to write some more on the article.

But first...Coffee.

I followed the smell of coffee that lingered in the air. I entered the kitchen, and I found Ben and Brendan brewing coffee and talking. I am glad that they are still friends, I wouldn't be able to handle it if they weren't talking to one another.

'Ah, Emma! You're awake!' exclaimed Ben as he rushed over and kissed my cheek. 'Did you sleep well?' he asked.

I gave Brendan a sidelong glance before answering, 'Yes, I did'

'That's funny because you still look tired...up late?' he questioned as my Ma would.

'Something like that...' I replied with a shy smile before walking over to Brendan and kissing him good morning.

'Did we wake you, my love?' asked Brendan sweetly.

'Technically, no. The coffee aroma did' I laughed.

'Of course!' our laughs blended into one, it was a beautiful sound. We even got Ben to laugh along with us.

'Emma! Stop laughing!' Ben laughed out.

When I was finally about to control my laugh a little better I asked, 'Why?'

'Because your laugh is contagious, as soon as anyone hears your laugh, everyone starts to laugh!' he laughed.

'Very true' I replied, unable to hold my laughter any longer.

Once we had our laughing fit and our coffee ready we headed to the living room, we spent most of the morning talking about the past year, like my wedding and Ben's work. But, unfortunately, Brendan had to go to work and Ben left to go and meet his uncle and aunt while he was in town. Leaving me at home.

Maybe I should write a little bit on my novel then go and visit Ma and Maybelle. After all, I have plenty of time to write my article. I thought to myself as I headed to my room to change into my day clothes, since the weather is warming up I can finally wear my dresses again.

As soon as I set out my daily plan, I got to writing my novel.

***

'Queen Julieanne? The King would like to see you' informed Roseanne from the doorway to my chambers.

'Thank you, Roseanne. I will be there shortly' I replied.

As I made my way to the meeting room, I couldn't help but wonder why he didn't just come to meet me.

'Ah, Darling, welcome!' exclaimed the King.

'Hello, Dear. What can I do for you'

'I wanted to see my beautiful wife and daughter'

'Well, your daughter is as happy to see you as I am'

'That is wonderful. It's not long now until we get to meet her'

'Four weeks left' I replied with a small, joyous smile 'And thankfully, everything has been arranged'

'Yes, well, you are giving birth to the next Princess of our Kingdom, therefore, she will play a crucial role in this Kingdom'

'Indeed she will' I replied, rubbing my belly.

'This baby is the future of our Kingdom, which is great, but also dangerous,' he started 'It is dangerous as this child will be the target of the other Kingdoms, they want my bloodline to leave the throne, if we bring this beautiful princess into this world, it will automatically make her a target'

'What are you saying?'

'I am saying that until the child is born, you are not to leave the castle, that includes going down into the villages. Once the princess is born, we will need extra staff to monitor the castle, and yourself. And since the princess will be with you at all times, it will mean that the guards will have to figure out a way to protect you both at all times. I am sure the word of the princess has already spread across the nation. So, we need to be careful'

'I was planning on doing all of that anyway'

'I know, but now it will happen either way. Your safety and our princesses is all that matters to me, Julieanne'

'I know,' I replied, smiling.

'Julieanne! I thought I told you to stay in your room!' bellowed Father.

'Chancellor! That is not your place!' the King bellowed back.

'Your Highness, the Queen is my daughter, she is to do as I say'

'She is your Queen, therefore, that outranks blood relations. She is here on my summoning. If you have a problem, please speak to me about it'

'Yes, Sir'

I don't think I have ever seen Father afraid of someone before, but he seems to be frightened of my husband.

'Father, I will be heading back to my room shortly' I replied, hoping to end the tension in the room.

'No, you are to stay here and help me prep the staffing for our princess'

'You seriously think it is a good idea to have Julieanne working and walking around while our enemies are lurking around waiting for the birth of the Princess?'

'I know I am your King. Julieanne is my Queen. I am positive that Julieanne will be safe alongside me, I have a guard surrounding this room. Chancellor, I trust you can see yourself out?' he asked.

'Yes, Sir' he replied, shooting me a furious glare.

'He doesn't like being denied something' I spoke, evenly.

'He needs to understand his place in
this Kingdom. Challenging us is not
an option. I don't know to what extent
my father allowed him to do while he
ruled, but this is now our Kingdom.
We make the rules, and I say that the
Chancellor needs to learn his place'

'I completely agree, but it is my
father. He doesn't like being told
what to do'

'You're worried that he will take his
anger out on you?'

'Well, of course, I am'

'Don't be. He isn't to be alone with
you anymore, he is also due to move
into the government building with the
other official members of Court'

'Ok…'

'Relax, my Queen. We will figure all of this out together'

'I do hope so, for the sake of our daughter' I replied, with my hand overlapping my husband's over our daughter.

I will do whatever it takes to keep my child alive and well, even if it means leaving my crown behind. And if it was to come to that I hope my husband will understand and resume his role as King. So he can make the Kingdom safe enough for me and the Princess to return home once again.

***

'Emma!' called Maybelle as I entered the house.

'Hey, Maybelle. Why aren't you at school?'

'Because she heard that you were coming over today, and decided that she was 'sick'' Ma interrupts.

'Oh...sorry about that' I replied, before turning my attention back to Maybelle 'You can not have a day off school if I am coming home, I will be here when you get home anyway...ok?'

'Fine'

'So, Emma. How are things going for you and Brendan?' Ma asked as she led me into the kitchen and started boiling the water for our coffee.

'Things are going well, the house is in the way we both want it. Brendan isn't grieving Clara's death anymore, instead, he is celebrating her life. And Ben's in town too'

'He is? When did he arrive?' she asked.

'Yesterday afternoon'

'I didn't know he was coming into town' she considered.

'Yeah, neither did I. Apparently, he didn't tell anyone that he was. He wanted to surprise everyone'

'Where is he staying?'

'With Brendan and I'

'Oh, that will be nice'

'Can I see Ben?' asked Maybelle as we were now sitting around the living room table.

'He is out today, maybe I can get him to stop over tomorrow or sometime before he leaves?'

'That would be fun, thank you' she replied.

'Maybelle, since you didn't go to school today, what are you expected to be doing?'

'Either school work or cleaning the house'

'Yes, and what does that not include?'

'Sitting down with you and Emma drinking coffee?'

'Yes, so what are you going to do?'

'Clean...but Ma—'

'No 'buts'. You wanted to stay home to see Emma, now you have seen her' Ma scolded.

'But that's not fair!' exclaimed Maybelle.

'Yes, it is. Once the school day is finished you can come out and talk with her, if she is still here'

'Fine!' she exclaimed before storming out of the room.

'She enjoys it when you visit, but she can not be taking days off school to see you. Especially, when she can visit you at any time'

'Yes, I know what you are saying. She is at mine more times than not, so I don't understand why she took today off'

'Neither do I. But since she did, I can not let the house rules slide. Otherwise, she will do this more often and that is something that I can not have'

'I understand that. Would you prefer me to call after she has already left for school?'

'That would be helpful'

Ma and I spent the afternoon talking about things that had happened, shortly before I left Maybelle came and sat with us, now that the school day was finished. Maybelle bombarded me with question after question. But eventually, I had to leave. Brendan was due to arrive home shortly.

Chapter Nineteen

I am well aware that people are going to disrespect my writing, send me threatening telegrams, tell me that I shouldn't have the right to write about it and so many more, since this is what happened when I wrote the article on the mining accident that killed a large population of my home town and it's surrounding towns, include my Pa. And that wasn't even a feminist article or an article on rights and equality. Therefore, I am expecting this article to bring me more backlash than my original

```
nationally recognised article ever
will.
```

Once I had finished writing and packing tea orders I could focus on cleaning the house and chatting with Ben as I did.

'How is the article coming along?' asked Ben as he swept the kitchen floors, the tiles were the easiest to sweep.

'I wrote a small paragraph this morning, I will end up writing more tomorrow' I replied as I washed the dishes.

'That's a good idea. I suppose the sooner you get it finished, the better'

'Yes, indeed. As then I will get other articles to write'

'Are you excited to publish the article?'

'A little, I am less excited for the backlash. But I will deal with that when it comes'

'I am sure you will' he started 'When does Brendan return home from the markets?'

'He should be back within the hour, he has agreed to help me clean out the backyard'

'Ok, cool'

'Do you have any plans for today?'

'No, I am helping you today'

'Maybe, later on, you could go and visit Maybelle and Ma? Maybelle was asking to see you yesterday'

'I suppose I can fit that in'

'Good, otherwise, Maybelle would kill me if I didn't ask you'

'That she would'

As we cleaned the house I realised that Brendan had left quite a bit of Clara's stuff out, unable to put everything into storage. And I liked that. It made the house feel cosier, and it made it feel like Clara was still here, watching over us. I am glad that we decided to leave some of her out where she left them, granted, most of her things were now in storage. Brendan didn't have the courage to donate or sell anything. So, now the attic is filled to the brim with Clara's stuff, all in boxes that are mounted on the wall, touching the ceiling.

I gently dusted all of the things that belonged to Clara, afraid that I would knock something off and it would smash, I don't know how Brendan would cope if I did that.

For the most part, this house has always felt like home. It was always a happy, loving, welcoming place to be. Even now.

But every now and again I am reminded of the horrors that took place within these walls for months on end. Brendan doesn't talk about those months, and what he had to endure. I couldn't imagine watching my Ma slowly die, so I couldn't even relate to him on that level. Pa died, sure. But at least I didn't have to watch him die. His death was quick, unlike Clara's. Clara deserved much more than what she got.

'What are you thinking about?' Ben asked, clearly my thought process was showing on my face.

'Clara'

'Oh, sorry'

'It's all good'

'How is Brendan coping with all that anyway?'

'He's getting there, slowly. As expected though, he has his days where he doesn't want to get out of bed, but other things he is up super early to get stuff done and keep his mind distracted'

'That must be hard for you'

'Sometimes, but I did the same thing with Pa's death. I understand why he is doing it and there is nothing I can say or do to relieve his pain. So, I just need to be here when he is ready to talk and move forward'

'Do you think that is going to be anytime soon?'

'From the way he has been lately, probably. He seems to be more relaxed, which is great. And he hasn't woken up at some early hour of the morning'

'Well, that sounds like progress'

'Yes, it is'

Cleaning the house has always calmed my thinking, it makes me more relaxed. Focused. With Ben being here helping me clean, it is a positive thing as I don't have to do it all alone, but it is also a negative as I am talking about things I would rather not be thinking about when I am cleaning. But, I do appreciate the company. Especially since it is Ben.

'I'm home!' called Brendan from the front door.

As I headed towards him and took some bags from him I asked, 'Were there many people out today?' Given the fact that today there is generally only a small market, in which not everyone goes.

'Yeah, it was busier than usual' he replied with a smile as he unpacked the bags with Ben and I.

'We can pack this away' suggested Ben, with a failed attempt to give Brendan a break.

'It's ok. And besides, you don't know where everything goes' he replied.

'Yes, but I can learn'

'True, but it will take longer with only you doing it, if I left here I would go out to the backyard and Em would join me'

'Maybe'

'But thank you for the thought' Brendan replied with a smile.

Once we finished packing everything away, we all headed out to clean the backyard. It is very much overdue.

As the day went on I could feel the winter air's bite hitting against my warm skin, my room is the coldest in the house, therefore, it is the first room to feel the crisp cold chill of the air. While my room is the coldest during the colder months of June, July, and August it is also the warmest room during the hotter months of December, January, and February. My room is by far the best in the house, especially for an avid reader and writer such as myself. While I do not have a fireplace I do have some warmer blankets. This helps me manage during the cold months.

I love winter, the cold, fresh air. The smell of rain, when it actually rains that is. My town isn't exactly known for rainy weather, however, the rainy season would be in winter, and other seasons don't tend to get as much rain. It is another reason I love winter. I love being able to stay inside, coffee or tea in hand while I work on my novel, or articles or read my favorite books. This is something that I adore doing and can do without getting too hot. And since it doesn't snow here, I don't have to worry about getting too cold.

***

'I am going to have a quick shower' announced Brendan before kissing me and heading upstairs.

'Ok,' I replied.

'Well, that took longer than I expected with three people,' Ben said calmly.

'Yeah, it did. But Brendan and I hadn't cleaned it for a little while, and the lawn needed a mow. That took the longest, I suppose'

'I would assume so. Are you coming with me to see Maybelle and your Ma?'

'No, I need to get more stuff done here. Besides, I was there yesterday. And Maybelle wants to see you'

'Ok, well I'll be home before supper'

'Thank you' I replied before Ben left me alone, standing in the cleaned house. I could hear the shower running, the only indication that someone was here with me. The house suddenly felt lonely and quiet.

I must be getting used to the continuous noise. I thought to myself as I headed to my desk, ready to begin writing my novel.

***

'Queen Julieanne?' spoke the guard
from the doorway of my chambers. I
don't know him.

'Yes?' I answered.

'I have been told to inform you that
I will be rotating shifts with the
other guard. Roseanne will continue
to guard you against within the room
and assist you with everything'

'Thank you,' I replied. How I hated
being locked away in the castle.

Shortly after the guard left me,
Roseanne entered the room.

'Roseanne, have you spoken to my
husband yet?'

'Yes, my Queen. He will be here shortly to check up on you'

'Thank you' I replied smiling.

'How are you going with the extra protection?' she asked with a small smile.

'It feels like I am being watched constantly'

'Well, I suppose you are. In theory'

'I don't like that very much. But I will do anything to protect my daughter'

'The Princess will have amazing parents and amazing protection. I doubt anything bad will happen to her. Especially with all of the constant protection' she spoke before taking a seat at the desk, preparing for her work.

'Why do you constantly work?' I started before correcting myself, 'I mean,

why do you continuously fill out
paperwork that you don't need to be
doing?'

'My Queen, someone needs to do it.
And since I am with you a lot of
the time it is only fitting that
I fill out the paperwork regarding
your protection. Besides, all of the
guards have to work to keep you safe.
I am here to help with protection,
yes, but also maid work. Since that
is my original job. But since the
Princess and you have become a much
bigger target for the other kingdoms,
I have begun training to be your
primary guard. Obviously, I will not
be able to be your only guard anytime
soon, but one day'

'I don't know what I would do without
you, Rose'

'My Queen, you will continue to do
great things. And your fire to help
people will only keep growing' she

started before shifting papers in her hands, 'You are the best Queen we have had'

'Besides the former Queen, she was the best'

'Yes, but you are even challenging her legacy'

'How thrilling'

'It is. Without the both of you, this Kingdom would only decrease in superiority. Which will only make the other kingdoms more inclined to destroy us. We may have the best protection, war ethics, and power. But we can still be overthrown. It was only a matter of time before one of the other kingdoms planned an attack

'They are all very valid points. But how do you know all of this? Most of this information is kept for myself, the King, and the members of the Court'

'I have been a maid in this castle for more years than I would like to admit. I hear all that happens within these walls. I am supposed to do my job quietly, no questions, and definitely not interrupt meetings and other private events. However, I am still required to supply you all with drinks and cleaning services throughout your meetings. So, I cannot help but listen'

'That is some interesting points. I might need to ensure that you are the only maid present during the meetings. I don't want anything bad to get in the hands of some of the maids, since some are quite the gossip. The last thing we need is to have a Kingdom that is in panic. They will not help us at all, especially if the Kingdom finds out about the threats of war and attacking us. We need the Kingdom to be prepared, not panicking'

```
'Yes, I understand. I can go over the
maid schedules and find out if there
is anything I can change?'
```

```
'That would be amazing'
```

***

'How's the book coming along?' asked Brendan from the doorway.

'*Novel*' I corrected with a smile. 'But, it is coming along nicely. I am really happy with it's plot and the directing the storyline and characters are heading'

'That's wonderful. Much more to write?'

'Well, that depends on when I deem the story should come to an end and when I am happy with it'

'I guess that makes sense. Publishing?'

'I would hope so. But in saying that, the general public doesn't approve of female novelists' I replied with a small, sad smile. 'But that is the unfair, misogynistic world we live in'

'Wow, calm down with the big words' he laughed.

Laughing, I rose from my seat at the desk and walked over to him. Instinctively he put his arms around my waist and pulled me close.

'I love big words' I whispered into his strong, broad chest.

'I know,' he replied, placing a kiss on my forehead.

I grow more in love with the man every day, I wouldn't change him in any way. He is my better half, my soulmate, my everything. My Ma has always told me that somewhere in this world is your soulmate, but until you actually meet that one person who changes you for the better, I didn't believe her. It's hard to believe in a soulmate or true love if you are blinded by other things, especially in a small town like my own. But I managed to find Brendan, I only hope that others can find their soulmates too.

'I could do with a coffee' I sighed before placing a loving, sweet kiss on his mouth.

'Hmmm,' he thought as he returned my kiss with one of his own. 'I think I can arrange that'

'Wonderful' I sighed before stepping out of his embrace and prepared to organise my office.

As I dawdle around my small office, I noticed that a number of things had been misplaced. Which only means one thing...

'Who has been in my office?!?' I called Brendan.

Shortly after I called him, he appeared in the doorway carrying my blissful, hot coffee. 'Was not me, so I am guessing Ben' he spoke as he passed my coffee to me.

'Why would Ben be in here?' I questioned, skeptically.

'Maybe he saw some of you writing and was fascinated?'

'Doubtful...there is nothing showing that he would see from the doorway'

'I am not too sure then. Did you have something of his?'

'No, I don't borrow things from him as I don't need to. We both have completely different writing styles, therefore, it wouldn't be any of his works'

'Hmm, then I definitely have no idea. He should be returning home soon'

'Ok...I'm going to go for a shower' I announced as I grabbed my mug and headed for the stairs.

'Call out if you need anything' Brendan replied before turning back towards the kitchen, opting out of talking to me about my office mystery.

Ben has no reason to go into my office, so why did he? I asked myself as I entered the bathroom.

I have always kept the bathroom clean. The basin is clear of products and all of the cords are tucked out of view.

I constantly find myself looking into the mirror and questioning things about my appearance. I am working on stopping that, especially, since it is not good for my mental health. When I do find myself looking into the mirror, I have to remind myself to pick one feature that I am happy with. And to try and not focus on all of my features that I am not happy with.

Everybody has doubts about themself, whether that is your appearance, skills, or tastes. That, unfortunately, doesn't tend to go away. But if you think of at least one positive thing about yourself or what you have achieved daily, it helps to balance out any issues or lack of confidence that you may have. Ma constantly tells me that it is normal to doubt yourself in one way or another, but if you can fight yourself and think about positive things instead, it makes it all easier. Every day, I have begun writing everything that I am thankful for down in a notebook, my emotions throughout the day, the things that have made me happy but also the things that have made me sad. This has been helping me cope with things and gives me a way to let emotions out of my head, so they are no longer weighing me down. I recommend this to everyone, even if you are not struggling currently.

The hot water feels magical on my tense shoulders. I didn't realise how much I needed this shower until I got in here and turned it on. The relaxation that this brings is insane.

Once I had finished in the shower, I headed downstairs to find Ben seated in the living room, sitting by the fireplace. I can feel the heat radiating off it in blasts, making me feel cosy and at home. The heat that the fireplace brings is something that will always make me think of reading a book or drinking tea alongside Maybelle or Ma.

'Ben, were you rifling through my office?' I questioned with a raised eyebrow.

'Yes...why?' he replied.

'What were you looking for?'

'Nothing really, just reading your works'

'Why didn't you just wait and ask if it was ok with me for you to go through my office and look at my writing?'

'I didn't think you would mind'

'But you don't know what I have in there or what I am writing'

'Do you have a problem with me reading your works?'

'Generally, no. But if you are going to go through my office without asking then, yes. I don't need someone staying in my house and touching my stuff without consulting me first'

'Did you want me to stay elsewhere?'

'No, of course I don't. But don't go through my stuff, especially my writing, by asking me first'

'Ok' he started, 'I'm going to go for a walk'

'It's dark and cold out'

'I will bring a light and a jacket' he replied before turning out of the living room.

Once I heard the front door slam shut, I knew he was gone. But the question is, when will he return?

'That went better than expected' interrupted B.

'Yes, I suppose it did. I am going to go up and read' I
announced before heading back towards my bedroom.

CHAPTER TWENTY

I am now on the last stretch of my article before publishing it to the national paper, hopefully, the backlash won't be too bad...hopefully.

I decided to add more to my article before heading off to bed last night, writing,

```
I am a proud feminist, who is not
afraid to speak up about what is right
and what is not. This article will
be a reflection on what I believe
```

to be right and compared to what the majority of our society believes to be right.

Stereotypically, a female in today's society is expected to bear children, be a housewife, and if they are lucky gain a job such as teaching, becoming a seamstress, becoming a nanny or a midwife or nurse. Whereas, the more strength-based, masculine jobs are left to the men in society.

Women have limited options on what they can do for a job, and that is if they are lucky enough to be given the opportunity. I strongly believe that women have the right to a job that they wish to have and that they shouldn't be stopped from reaching for these goals, currently, these goals are unrealistic dreams and feeble hopes. The right to a job of your choosing shouldn't be based on gender, it should be based on knowledge, interests, and dreams. If a female wishes to work in the mines then they shouldn't be stopped. And if a man decided that they wanted to become a teacher, why should they be frowned upon? Why is it that society has the jurisdiction to decide what an individual does with their own life?

Our government has sovereignty over what both the sexes can and cannot do. Due to the dominion that the government holds over our society, it extremely limits the boundaries that people are able to push without facing serious consequences for their actions. The government has the ultimate power, therefore, they have the ultimate say in whether or not both sexes have the right to the same things. Instead of fixing the inequality between the sexes, the government is determined to ensure that the ideologies and prejudice are maintained throughout generations, without change or individuals challenging them on these. The government has become used to individuals just sitting back and letting them do their own thing, and for those that haven't noticed, our government doesn't have one single female representative. No one to formally speak up on behalf of women's rights or equal rights between both sexes.

For those that are unaware, feminism is the firm belief that both sexes deserve to be equals, and that you stand up for and advocate for women's rights. While feminism means different things to different individuals, this is the underlying belief system of the movement. The feminist movement is gaining more and more followers daily, but some are too afraid to speak up for what they believe in. No person should ever be denied the right to speak up, to use their voice to influence change.

Another thing that we, as a society need to change is the equal rights to an education, equal pay, and equal opportunities given to both of the sexes.

The rights of every individual matter, every voice matters, and every whisper matters.

To summarise this article,

Women deserve respect.

Women deserve to be heard.

Men and women both deserve equal rights and opportunities.

Women deserved to be paid the same amount as their male counterparts.

Everyone- no matter your gender- deserves an education.

No sex is superior to the other. No sex should have more rights than the other.

Our society needs to start treating all individuals with the same amount of respect, love, and admiration.

Both sexes deserve gender equality.

Written by,

Emma Hicks/Smith

I hope that this article inspires others to speak up and give themselves a voice that they deserve to be heard.

Everyone deserves and has the right to freely express their dreams, thoughts, and beliefs to others around them, whether they are female or male. Equality should be the foundation of our world, not inequality. Inequality is something that we all face daily, no matter our place or lifestyle in this world. I know there will always be inequality in this world, but I also know that this would be a much greater and worthwhile place if equality was focused on and supported by all.

'Em?' called Brendan, causing me to lose my train of thought.

'Yes, B?' I called back.

Appearing in the bedroom, B continued with,

'Have you completed that article for the national paper yet?'

'Yes, I completed it last night, how come?' I asked, placing my novel, *The Feminine Mystique,* on the bed and looking at Brendan.

'I wanted to know if you wanted me to drop it by the publishing house?'

'Are you heading into town?'

'I will be meeting with a friend shortly. I guessed that you would want to read some more of your book since you have been preoccupied with other stuff lately'

'Ok, sure. Thank you' I replied. 'It's sitting on my desk in the office, it should be the first one that you see'

'Awesome, I'll see you when I get back. Enjoy your book'

'Thanks, B' I replied with a small smile.

***

It has been two days since Ben got called back to work, thankfully, he didn't rifle through any more of my stuff. Which I was very relieved about. I have never liked it when people go through my stuff without asking, I feel like it is disrespectful and rude.

Shortly after I finished reading for the day and went downstairs to the living room to start the fire, Brendan waltzed through the front door.

'In here' I called, allowing B to follow my voice further into the house.

'Did you drop it by the publishing house?' I asked as I sat down in my chair, meticulously placed in front of the fire.

'Yes, all submitted' he replied, taking a seat in his own chair.

'How was your visit?' I asked.

'It went well, I haven't seen some of them for quite some time, since they have been away visiting relatives'

'That's good'

'How's your book coming along?'

'It's a novel, but it is just about finished'

'That's awesome, will you publish it?'

'Probably not, but I hope too. I think it would be really cool to do, but you know how to the general public is about female writers, and unfortunately, mine is in that dislike'

'It won't be a thing forever, they are bound to let women publish books using their own names and not a male name'

'You would think so, but with our government, I don't like the chances'

'I suppose. If it was allowed, would you publish?'

'Yes, if I knew my novel was going to reach my viewers then yes, I would consider it'

'Why don't you just publish under a male name?' Brendan asked curiously.

'Why would I elect to use a name that isn't who I am and is not someone I would want to become? If I am going to write the book, I am going to use my name. It is my name, I have the right to use it wherever I want. I am not going to hide behind some fake persona just because people disagree with female authors'

'That's completely fair. But if it was the only way you would ever be able to publish it, would you consider it?'

'No'

'So, you just wouldn't publish it at all?'

'Correct, under no circumstance will I ever give in to the prejudices of our society. In fact, I will continue to disagree and go against those that do. That is the only way we will make change'

'I have no doubt in my mind that you will fight for what you believe in. That is one of the many reasons that I love you'

'Thank you, I love you too'

Half an hour later, Maybelle waltzed into the room, clearly forgetting to knock at the front door.

'Hey, Belle, did you forget to knock?' I asked with a knowing smile.

'No, I didn't forget. I just couldn't be bothered' she replied with her own smile.

'It's good to see you, May,' interrupted Brendan.

'It's good to see you too, Brendan'

'Look at you guys, giving each other nicknames and talking' I laughed.

'So, Belle, what can I do for you?' I asked.

'I got bored so I thought I might stop by and see if you needed anything' she replied, 'I like the name Belle too' she continued with a smile that met her eyes, making them glisten in the afternoon light.

'I've been calling you that for months' I replied.

'Yes, but still'

'Ok...well, I don't think there is anything that you can really do today. But you are more than welcome to stay around'

'Thank you, did you finish that article that you were writing?'

'Yes, submitted it this morning'

'Oh, so you will be receiving more telegrams and stuff soon?'

'Yes, most likely once it is published'

'Oh...'

'Don't worry, May. It will all be ok...people can be cruel, but that doesn't mean that Em is going to be upset or stop writing...ok?' comforts B.

'Yeah...I guess'

'It will be ok, Belle. I promise...' I replied, comforting her as I rose and pulled her into an embrace.

I never thought about how any of this would impact May-belle and Ma. But it should be ok...I hope. I thought as I held Maybelle, until eventually, I released her from my grasp.

'Emma?' asked Maybelle, cautiously.

'Yes?' I replied.

'Will you come to me if you need someone to talk to?'

'Of course, I would, but it would also depend on what I needed to talk about'

'Yeah, I know that. I'd come to you too'

'I'm glad,' I smiled.

***

The Incident of the Lost Dog

This will be a very brief article, I have intended this article to include all important information.

Our dearest, Poppy Hargrave, has lost her precious dog, Annie. Annie is a border collie that was last seen on the outskirts of town, on Mrs. Hargrave's property.

If anyone has seen Annie, please visit Poppy and let her know where and when, or if anyone has got Annie at their house, please, please, please return her to her beloved family. They are missing Annie dearly.

If anyone else has further information on Annie's whereabouts please either see myself or Poppy.

Written By:

Emma Smith

That has got to be one of the smallest articles I have ever written. I thought to myself as I placed the article to the side, ready to start writing my novel.

***

It has been almost 6 months since the birth of the Princess, and almost 3 months since we won the battle against the Kingdom's trying to get to the Princess.

'Julieanne?' called Roseanne.

'Come in, Roseanne' I called back, 'You know that you do not need to knock right? If the door is unlocked, then you are welcome to enter' I continued once she entered the room.

'I know, you have informed me before'

'Yes, indeed I have. But you still seem to knock'

'Yes, I do as you are my Queen'

'But I am also a friend. My friendship with you will always come before my duties as Queen. Now, Amelia has just gone down for her nap in the nursery'

'Ok, I shall be quieter then, I don't wish to wake her'

'Trust me, she won't be sleeping for long. I swear, that child only sleeps for half an hour at a time'

'That sounds hard'

'It is, but Phillips and I will manage. As we don't really have a choice'

'I'd be happy to watch over her if you have other things you need to be attending?'

'I guess that would be ok, now that the threats have all been neutralised for now and there is peace back to the Kingdom...'

'Don't worry, she will be ok'

'I know she will, but I'm worried about you. Amelia is an Angel, but when she is angry she acts like the Devil'

'I shall keep that in mind, now go and find the King'

'Ok...'

As I walked through the castle, I was relieved to find all of the extra guards had left. The castle seems at peace like the rest of the Kingdom. Since we took the war to the invading Kingdoms, rather than fighting them in my Kingdom and having to deal with the carnage ourselves and putting my people at risk, the council decided that it would be best to go out inside of waiting for them inside the walls.

A lot of men from the villages joined the battle, all of whom wanted to keep the Princess safe. I thanked them all dearly and supplied their families with money and food that would last them years to come.

Two months ago, we had a ceremony celebrating and mourning those who died fighting for myself and Amelia. Those names will be added to a wall in the main town where they will be recognised and respected for years to come.

'Ahhh, Darling!' exclaimed Phillips as he saw me and walked over to join me. As soon as he noticed that I was missing something, his smile quickly faded to a frown with worry creased upon his face. 'Where's Amelia?' he asked, failing to hide the fear in his voice.

'Relax, dear. She is with Roseanne. They are both safe'

'You left Amelia with your maid?'

'Yes, Roseanne is a dear friend, and she did so much for Amelia and I during the war. She even learned to fight so she could protect us herself'

'Yes, I am aware. But she is also a maid'

'For now, yes. But I actually wanted to talk to you about that. If you have a minute?'

'Always, for you I do' he replied smiling, his worry vanishing and is now replaced with love.

I never thought Phillip and I would have a normal marriage, but as the days turned into years we grew stronger together, and soon we grew to love each other fiercely. Nothing will be able to stop us from protecting our people and our small, growing family. For now, I am content with Phillip, Amelia, and Roseanne. Well, I guess, the former king and my father were also in there somewhere.

My love for my people and my family is timeless…

***

'Brendan!' I called from my office.

'Yes?' he replied, appearing in the doorway.

'Guess what'

'What?' he asked with a sly smile.

'I finished my novel!' I squealed.

'REALLY!?!?' he exclaimed.

Nodding, I jumped up from my chair and ran into his open arms, feeling his arms around me made me feel invincible.

'Em, we need to celebrate!' he announced.

'Yes! What did you have in mind?' I asked, excitedly.

'It's a surprise!' he answered as he dragged me to the front door, leading me into the unknown.

Chapter Twenty-One

A week after I finished writing my novel, which I decided to name, Untamed Julieanne. I am absolutely obsessed with the novel and the storyline, I am also missing my world. I have decided that I will talk with Edwardson about publishing my book and let him know that I will not use a male name in order to publish it.

I have also published my article in the national paper, in which I have already received 50 telegrams and some have also been sent to the publishing house. I have a new batch that I am yet to open that came in the mail today, Brendan has just left and headed to the mines for the day. But before I open the next batch of telegrams, I will be replying to some of the ones that I have already opened, some of which are from friends and family.

First on my very long list is Ben,

Dearest Benny,

Thank you for your telegram!

I am getting bombarded with telegrams about my article, but no matter what they say, I am very proud to have published it. I appreciate your support and your defending me, but please be careful not to get into trouble with your boss. I would hate for you to get fired over me and this article. I will be spending my day replying and opening telegrams, I won't be replying to them all but only the ones that I think deserve or require a response from me.

Edwardson has gone on a week's break, I think that was mainly because he needed to refresh before being bombarded with telegrams and complaints, since he is the boss of the company they all get sent directly to him. Therefore, when he returns there will be a stack for him to go through. I will be sending him a telegram today to where he is staying in regards to the telegrams and if he would be able to help me publish my novel.

Once again, thank you for your support of my novel. I don't think I would have ever finished it without you, Brendan, Maybelle, and Ma. So, therefore, I owe you so much.

Amongst the telegrams, I have received a number of positive ones addressing things that I have mentioned. Mostly from females, however, surprisingly, I have received a couple from males who agree with what I am saying. That was something that I did not expect at all.

Anyway, since I have so much more to write today, I will be ending this telegram shorter than I would have liked.

I hope you are well and that you stay well, look after yourself.

Love yours,

Emma

One down, loads more to go. Next on my list was a young girl from Western Australia.

Dear Opal,

Thank you for your kind words of encouragement and gratitude.

I was very thrilled to have read your telegram after so many negative ones that I had received over the week that the article had been submitted. Your kind words mean the world to me.

I am so happy that you agree with what I have written! I was hoping to find females and males alike who agree with what I believe to be wrong and right. It is a big thing to write out against such big things in our society, but I have no regrets about doing so.

Please speak out about your beliefs, don't be afraid to. While there will always be negative outcomes to writing and speaking up, there will also be so many positive outcomes!

I look forward to hearing about your challenges and your voice in the future, please do not hesitate to send me a telegram!

Best wishes,

Emma Smith

I love getting telegrams like Opal's, they remind me of what I am aiming for. Without people like her, I am not sure I would continue fighting for all of the things that I do.

Now, I just need to write the telegram to Edwardson.

Dear Edwardson,

Great time for you to go away, otherwise you would be drowning in telegrams like myself.

In regards to the telegrams, did you want me to go through them and dispose of the ones that aren't relevant and keep those that are? I would be happy to do so since you have helped me so much when it came to publishing it for the paper, I wouldn't be here without you.

Also, as you are aware, I have completed my novel and have finished editing it. If possible, I would be keen to publish it (under my name, of course). I have also decided to stay with the newspaper if you are able to assist me in publishing it. This way you are ensuring that the newspaper is expanding to also publish novels, and as time goes on you would be one of the first to publish authors' works that are written by a female. Please, accept this. I have sent over my draft to the newspaper and it is sitting on your desk, waiting for your arrival home.

I wish you the best with your break and safe travels home.

I look forward to your reply,

Thank you,

Emma

Right, coffee time...

As I made my way through the house, toward the kitchen, I couldn't help but wonder how my novel would impact those that read it. It's a lovely story, and anyone could read it if they so desire. Those who agree with my writing in the newspaper will most likely read my novel since they have already accepted that I am a female novelist. But I guess we will have to see how many people will actually read it and how many people will be sending me telegrams of disapproval.

Once I had made my coffee, I returned to open up the telegrams that arrived today.

The first one read,

Emma Smith,

Why on earth would you write stuff like that? You aren't even supposed to be writing at all!

If you think this article will change anything, then think again! It won't! It is riddled with lies, I don't know how you sleep at night. Your family must be so disappointed in you.

Absolutely disgraceful!

-Unknown

'How on earth do I sleep at night?' I asked myself out loud.

'That's a question I'd ask myself too' spoke a voice from behind me, scaring me half to death.

'MAYBELLE!?' I screamed before continuing, 'How on earth did you get inside? The doors are locked, and last I checked you do not have a key" I asked, quizzically.

'I borrowed Ma's. I didn't mean to scare you. What are you reading?' she asked, directing my attention back to the heap of paper on my desk.

'Just some telegrams'

'Oh...may I come in?' she asked.

'Sure'

'Anything good?'

'Yes, I have found a couple that have been amazing, but then there are others that are cruel'

'I thought there would be some'

'Of course, there are always some. No matter what you are writing about'

'That's a really good point, I think that there shouldn't be any negative ones, as that is just going to upset the author'

'I definitely agree, but unfortunately, it won't change anytime soon, therefore we need to accept it and move on'

'That's true...'

'So, what are you here for?' I asked.

'Oh, right! Ma wanted to know if you had any teas and soaps in stock?' she replied.

'Yep, I made I new batch two days ago, and will make some more over the coming days'

As we made our way towards the back shed (where the soaps and teas are made) I couldn't help but wonder how much the world would change if people just stopped judging others or making others feel horrible, would it be better or worse?

'Which ones does she want?' I asked as we headed inside.

'She doesn't know, all she said was that she wants your most popular stock'

'Ok...' I started as I grabbed a bag and started loading the popular ones into it. 'Let her know that she doesn't have to pay for any of them' I continued once all items were in the bag.

'She won't like that'

'I know she won't, but I don't want her to pay. Therefore, she won't be'

'Ok, I'll let her know' she replied before hugging me and heading back towards the front lawn.

I wonder why Ma didn't stop by with her. I thought to myself as I headed back to the office to write a reply.

Once I returned to the office, I got straight to work.

Dear Reader,

I am sorry that you think that, it must make your life very boring and uneventful.

I will always speak up about things that I believe to be right or wrong, and unfortunately for you, that will never change. I love using my voice to empower others, clearly, you disagree with my choices. But fortunately for me, I am not after anyone's opinion or judgment.

I know that I am helping so many people, women and men alike. I stand for both sexes and all cultural differences.

As stated in my article, feminism is about equality, but not just that, it is important in so many ways and can help improve so many lives. So please, if you are planning to be anti-feminist, or anti-change, then please, think about how you act and what you say or write before doing it.

Thank you,

Emma Smith

'Hey, Em'

'Hey, B. Your home early' I stated.

'Yeah, they didn't need me to stay and pack up'

'Oh...ok'

'What are you writing?'

'I'm replying to a telegram from an unknown individual who disagrees with female novelists, female rights, and feminists as a whole. I am explaining some facts to him'

'Oh, that poor soul,' he replied with a wicked smile.

'Definitely' I laughed.

'What would you like to have for supper?' I asked Brendan.

'Umm, maybe just some sort of pasta?' he questioned.

'That sounds lovely, and I have all of the ingredients here'

'Amazing,' he spoke as he walked up behind me and wrapped his strong arms around my waist. '*What type of pasta were you thinking?*' he whispered into my ear before placing a trail of kisses down my neck.

'Umm, maybe spaghetti, I think'

'Mmmm'

'Unless you had something else in mind?'

'No...' he began as he continued his kissing trail, *'Well, at least not dinner'* he spoke wickedly as he pulled me back towards the bedroom.

***

The smell of coffee woke me from my slumber, the best thing to smell in the morning.

'Who's making coffee?' asked a sleepy Brendan from next to me, clearly last night's activities had left him tired.

'I'll go and investigate, you stay here' I replied, placing a small kiss on his lips before heading out towards the kitchen.

Every day I am here, married to Brendan, it just seems to be getting better and better. We rarely argue or fight, we don't often disagree with each other and we love spending time with each other and our family and friends. I couldn't ask for a better partner in crime.

Standing in the doorway to the kitchen, I spoke softly, *'Ma, what are you doing here?'*. I still managed to scare her, clearly she did not hear me coming.

'Emma! You scared me!' she hissed, glaring at me.

'Why are you in my house?' I asked, trying to keep my voice low so Brendan would be able to sleep in longer.

'I wanted to make you and Brendan some coffee since you refuse to accept any money from me!' she snapped.

'So, you came into my house without warning, at 7:30 am to make coffee because I wouldn't accept your money as payment for the soaps and teas?'

'Yes, I thought it would be a nice surprise for you and Brendan. You guys could have breakfast in bed and neither of you would need to leave the room to make it' she elaborated.

'Well, thank you. But please, for future reference, let me know that you will be stopping by so that I don't think someone is breaking in'

'Fine, now get back to bed and let me finish what I started'

'*As you wish, Ma*' I replied and headed back to the room.

Brendan looks so peaceful sleeping there, I don't remember the last time I actually saw him sleeping. He is almost always awake before me, to either go to work or make me coffee. It's nice to see him so relaxed and at ease.

'*Are you going to come back to bed or are you just going to watch me sleep?*' he spoke sleepily.

'*Right, Ma is in the kitchen making breakfast and coffee for us*' I whispered back.

'*Why?*'

'*Because I wouldn't let her pay me for the soaps and teas she got from me yesterday*' I replied, snuggling up against him.

'*So she snuck into our house to make us breakfast?*'

'*It appears so...*'

'*Ok...*'

After that point, I had no hopes of actually falling back to sleep, but I was quite content in lying with B while Ma cooked breakfast. It was relaxing and made me think that there is nothing wrong in the world, even though I know that there is so much wrong, there is also so much good.

I don't know how long I lay there in B's arms, but it felt like a lifetime. Eventually, Ma appeared in the doorway carrying a tray with our breakfast and coffee. Gently, I nudged Brendan awake.

'I tried delaying coming back in for a while, but if I waited much longer the eggs, bacon and coffee would have gotten cold. I also can't stay any longer, since Maybelle will be waking up soon' explained Ma as she entered and handed me the tray.

'That's fine, thank you for coming over,' I replied.

'Thank you for not kicking me out'

'I would never kick you out, you would ground me for months' I laughed.

'Indeed, I would. Well, I'm off. I'll talk to you later, enjoy your breakfast' she replied, placing a kiss on my head and patting Brendan on the arm.

'Thanks, Mrs Hicks' mumbled Brendan before taking a sip of his coffee.

Not long after Ma left I decided to take a quick shower while Brendan finished his coffee, since he doesn't have to work at the mines today, he is taking his sweet time to enjoy it. Which I most certainly do not begrudge him for.

Once I had completed my shower, I got to work writing my latest task.

Winter's Upon Us

Once again, the cold bliss of winter has rested its grip on our beautiful town. This means it is time to bring

out the light jumpers, start the fireplace, and snuggle with loved ones.

Personally, I believe that winter is
a time to rejoice and reminisce about
the year thus far, allowing ourselves
the time to refresh our minds and
relax in our homes. While this can
be easily debated against, this is my
personal opinion which I will stand
by.

Please be mindful, that as lovely as
our winter is, you are still able to
get a cold and other illnesses that
spread rapidly through our little
town. Please be advised that if you
are feeling unwell, please stay home
and tend to yourself before going
out in public. For the parents, this
is a great time to spend time with
their children, especially since no
night work is permitted during this

```
season. Therefore, nightfall is the
best time to spend quality time with
your family.
```

```
I hope everyone is enjoying the winter
bliss as much as I am!
```

```
Written by,

Emma Hicks
```

Now with that over and done with, I can move forward
with my day.

Today, I am going to edit an article before publishing, read
and respond to some of the telegrams, and then spend the
rest of the day with Brendan. Since he is generally working

most of the time we don't get to spend much time together. While I get my editing, reading, and replying done he
has decided to clean the house. Even though I cleaned it
two days ago.

CHAPTER TWENTY-TWO

*D*earest Em,

I had to leave early this morning, as I have been asked to cover the early shift at the mines. I promise I will be home before the party this afternoon.

I have left a little something on the bench for you, I hope you love it.

My darling, I can't wait to spend all afternoon with you. I know I agreed to not work on your birthday, however, they needed someone in the morning, and since it wasn't a long shift I thought it would be ok, and the extra money always helps too.

I love you so much, and I can't wait to see your smiling face once I return home. The party is going to be amazing, I cannot believe you are turning 20 this year, it's insane. That means I have spent 5 birthdays alongside you, and I wouldn't have it any other way.

You are my entire world. My entire being. My one and only. My everything.

Love (Forever yours) B xx

I'm not even mad that he left so early this morning, or that he left on my birthday. This note is beautiful, I cannot believe he is mine. I thought.

Ring...ring...ring...

I swear, that telephone never stops ringing.

'Hello?' I answer.

'Happy Birthday, Emma!' called Ma and Maybelle from the other end of the line.

'Thanks!' I exclaimed back, 'Are you both still coming to the party this afternoon?'

'Absolutely, we wouldn't miss it for the world'

'Wonderful'

'What are you doing this morning?'

'I am writing a quick article for the national newspaper, addressing some minor things'

'Oh, on your birthday?'

'Yes, I need to get it done, there is no rest for me'

'I can see that, well, we will catch you this afternoon. I love you, Emma, don't work too hard'

'Thanks, Ma. I love you too, goodbye'

'Goodbye'

Right, I suppose I should get to work then. I thought as I headed to the office.

Protect Your Own

I am writing this to all of the people who have been sending me disrespect- ful, nasty telegrams in regard to my previous article, *The Ideology of the Prejudice World we Live in*. This arti- cle sparked quite a few individuals' disrespectful behaviors. In regards to them, by all means, have your say, but please keep those opinions to yourself or to your friends and families. Do not target them at me, as you aren't achieving anything. The things that are being said have not impacted me at all, so you are wasting your time. It is sad really, that so many people want to send telegrams to me to make themselves feel better about what I wrote. I have since replied to a few of them addressing that their opinion is just sad and something that I don't fully understand.

While I have been receiving quite a large number of negative comments and views on my article, I have also received numerous positive ones. For those that have sent me a positive telegram, thank you! I have sent out my replies to those telegrams, so I hope they find you all well and healthy.

For those that are scared to send me a telegram, that believe in what I have written, don't be. I have had so much joy reading what people have written about my article, I enjoy reading different people's views on the issues addressed and their experiences.

For those that disagree, thank you for not sending me telegrams. Move on, and move forward.

Written by:

Emma Smith

Right, now that's done. Edwardson won't receive it until he returns home in two days. I received a telegram from him a couple of days ago. Stated that he would assist me in editing and publishing my novel, he also stated that it would take a year or so to work it all out, hoping for less though. But he needs to finalise a couple of things prior to editing or publishing the novel. And we still need to design a cover. He is certain that we will publish it though, which is all I need to know for now.

'Oh! B's Present!' I exclaimed to myself. How on earth did I forget?

Once I arrived in the kitchen, I saw a perfectly wrapped box with a small fabric bow tied to the top., with a small note that read,

Happy Birthday, Em! Love B xx

Small yet, sweet.

Meticulously, I opened the wrapping paper, careful not to damage the present. Curiously, I peeped inside.

I opened the box and took out two wrapped up items. The first smaller item included a small necklace heart pendant with the inscription of an E and B. And the second item included a classic novel *Beauty and the Beast*, a novel that I absolutely adore and have another copy of. I feel like *Beauty and the Beast* shows us that you can't possibly judge someone from their appearance and that beauty truly lies from within. And I can also relate to Belle's obsession with reading, making the character relatable in more than one way. Having a personal connection to the characters helps build the liking and the adoration of the novel.

After placing my new pendant on my necklace, I grabbed the novel and headed for my room. My bookshelf is steadily growing, and I am loving every second of it. All of the novels that I read have some sort of significance to me or portray strong female leads. Most of the authors are female, however, I do have a couple that were written by a male.

Maybe I should read some more telegrams? I thought as I headed towards the office.

Emma,

I am sending you this telegram to thank you for writing your article. I showed it to my daughter and she loves it too. Everything that you wrote is the truth, you don't get many writers who are honest. I think that it is important to write the truth and to speak it.

You are fearless, bold, and determined to make things right. Thank you for giving my daughter hope for the future.

-Kiarra

Awww, thanks Kiarra. I thought.

I love reading these sorts of telegrams, they remind me of why I am the person I am and why I write what I write. I am also very glad that I didn't open a negative telegram today too.

'Emma? Are you here?' called Brendan from the front door.

'Office!' I called back.

Smiling, Brendan waltzed over and gracefully placed a small kiss on my lips.

'Happy birthday' he mumbled against my mouth before pulling away and pulling me from my chair into an embrace.

'Thanks, B' I started, hugging him tightly, 'Thank you for my presents' I continued.

'I notice that you are wearing the pendant'

'Yep, I sure am' I replied, touching the pendant softly.

'And the book is where exactly?'

'On my shelf with my other copy of *Beauty and the Beast*. It is a beautiful edition that you found'

'I knew you would love it'

'I do, thank you' I replied before kissing him again, 'I suppose we should start getting ready for the party'

'Hmmm...yeah, that's a great idea'

***

'EMMA! You're here!' cried Maybelle as I entered the room, hand in hand with Brendan. There are a lot more people here than I thought there would be.

'Sure am' I replied with a smile, dropping Brendan's hand to pull Maybelle into a tight, loving hug.

'Your crushing me'

'I know,' I laughed, releasing her.

Laughing we all headed towards the drinks.

Brendan really outdone himself with this party. I thought as I looked around at all of the small details.

'Did you do all of this yourself?' I asked him when he handed me a drink.

'I had some help' he smiled back as he gestured to the rest of the people in the room, 'I think most of the town chipped in where they could. It made it all a lot easier that is for sure'

'I'm glad,' I smiled.

'Emma, come over here!' exclaimed Ma. I'd somehow managed to walk straight past her without realising it.

'Hey Ma, I'm so glad you and Maybelle could make it'

'We wouldn't miss this, even if the world was ending' she replied, placing a small kiss on my cheek.

'Thank you' I returned a kiss to her cheek.

Looking around at the small crowded room, I couldn't be happier. Everyone who has ever supported, loved, and helped me is in this room. I wouldn't be who I am without them and that is something I am truly thankful for.

Ma, Maybelle, and Brendan are all here. It makes me feel so much happier.

'Emma?' spoke a male voice behind me. Whirling around to see who it was, and having to catch myself from screaming his name.

'Ben!' I exclaimed, 'What are you doing here!' I asked, shocked.

'I wouldn't miss your birthday for the world. Of course, I would come. Besides, this wouldn't be a party without me now would it?' he laughed.

Laughing, I replied, 'How did you get off work?'

'They owed me a favour from last year, I took them up on it and they couldn't say no'

'I bet they were furious'

'They were, but then I explained why I needed to come home, they decided it was a worthy cause. And since they read your articles, they quite liked your writing. I think that helped a bit'

'I can't believe that you are here!'

'Come on! Let's dance!' he exclaimed and dragged me to the middle of the floor and started dancing. The others all followed suit.

At that moment, I knew that I would never be alone. I had my family, that's what they all were. This town is my family, my home.

About the Author

Jasmin Rose is currently living in Newcastle, NSW Australia with her beloved family. She loves to read, write, review, and create art. Jasmin is currently working on her next novel. She loves spending time with her family, friends, and animals.

Jasmin decided to write this novel throughout 2023 in hopes that it inspires, encourages, and helps her readers. She is forever grateful for all that her family and friends have done for her, and continue to do. She is currently working towards owning her own bookstore, which is currently online, called Bookish Dreams.

Follow her journey on *Facebook, Instagram, and Tiktok* under *Jasminrosewrites*!

Signed copies, exclusive prints, bookmarks, and more will be featured on her Etsy storefront, Jasminrosewrites and her Shopify Store, Bookish Dreams.